getting THERE

D0907504

LYN DENISON

Bella
BOOKS
2011

Bella Books, Inc.
P.O. Box 10543
Tallahassee, FL 32302

Printed in the United States of America on acid-free paper
First published 2011

Editor: Anna Chinappi
Cover Designer: Linda Callaghan

ISBN 13: 978-1-59493-253-3

Other Bella Books by Lyn Denison

Always and Forever
Dream Lover
Dreams Found
The Feel of Forever
Gold Fever
Past Remembering

For Glennie
My LT
For putting up with me all these wonderful years

For Gayle R for her encouragement
And to the wonderful readers
who have contacted me
to tell me they've enjoyed my books,
I thank you muchly…

CHAPTER ONE

"There are no straight highways in life you know."

Katrin Oldfield murmured noncommittally as she picked up the coffeepot.

"And," continued her friend Em, "you are definitely at a fork in your road."

"A fork in my road? Do you think?" Kat asked with a faint smile.

"Mmm." Em nodded her head and her dark curls danced. "And it's a major fork. You have to make a choice. A very important choice."

"Choice?" Kat grimaced. "Can we not use the choice word? I have all sorts of trouble with that particular word."

"It's not the word, it's the action. Choice with a capital C." Em nodded knowingly. "Oh, yes, good old choices. We all have to make them."

Kat noisily stirred sugar into her friend's coffee.

"We don't always make good choices either," Em continued.

"Okay, Em. Enough. You don't have to tell me I make bad choices. I'm the queen of bad choices. I acknowledge that." Kat placed two mugs of coffee on the table and sat down opposite her friend. "Now, can we change the subject? Have a TimTam. They're your favorites."

"What makes you think chocolate biscuits are going to distract me?" Em reached out for one of the cookies. She took a bite and murmured appreciatively. "Mind you, it wouldn't be difficult." She took another bite. "Have you tried drawing your coffee up through your biscuit?"

Kat looked askance.

"You nibble a bit off the top. Then you nibble a bit off the bottom. Dip the bottom in your coffee and draw the coffee up through the biscuit. When your fingers get warm you pop the biscuit in your mouth. It's just," Em sighed, "divine."

"It sounds extremely messy to me."

"It can be if you're not quick enough. You see, it's all in the timing. But believe me, Kat, it's definitely better than sex. No false advertising there."

Kat laughed softly and shook her head. "Sounds intriguing, but I think I'll stick with the traditional." She chose a cookie. "But they're very more-ish, I'll give you that. Have you tried the new flavors? Double chocolate? Chewy caramel?"

"I'm not distracted, Kat. But good try. Now, we were talking about you."

"Far too boring at the moment, Em. In fact, far too boring, period."

"Are you kidding? Boring is not a word anyone would ever use in conjunction with you, Kat. Or me, for that matter. We are a couple of the world's more interesting people, wouldn't you say?"

Kat shook her head skeptically. "You are such a drama queen!"

Em gave a regal wave of her hand. "I know I am. But, that aside, I'm still your best friend. Would I lie to you?"

Kat laughed again. "Well, you are my best and oldest friend and you're nothing if not honest. Some would say that occasionally you're brutally honest."

"Now, now, Kat! Brutal is stretching it. But okay, it's settled that I'm honest, and I'm telling you you aren't at all boring. So. Now we can talk about your bad choices."

Kat rubbed at the rainbow flag insignia on her coffee mug. "I'm not sure I'm up to that today. I feel down enough without more verbal self-flagellation."

Em raised her eyebrows. "Wait while I process that. Have you got a dictionary handy?"

"You know what I mean, Em. I feel bad about how my life's going at the moment. Can't you just let me wallow for a while?"

"It's not healthy."

"I'm healthy as a horse."

"We're talking emotional health here."

"I'm not doing emotional at the moment, Em. Too stressful. And I'm too tired."

"I know, love," Em commiserated. "But you can't let broken relationships do this to you."

"My life is broken relationships. A whole string of them."

"Kat, you're thirty-four years old, and you've had two broken relationships. That's not bad. I had four before I found Joe."

"Yes, but you were the breaker. I'm the broken. It makes a difference."

"Mmm." Em gave that some thought. "Okay. Now who's being brutally honest?"

"I didn't mean—"

Em waved another chocolate biscuit. "I know what you meant. And there's a lesson here. You need a relationship where you call all the shots for a change. It's time for some meaningless sex."

Kat's eyes widened. "Mary Margaret Martin, what are you saying? Your mother would wash your mouth out with soap."

"Jeez, Kat. Don't even think about telling her what I said. She'll torture me for years. At least I didn't use the F-word."

"You never do, goody two-shoes."

Em stuck out her tongue at Kat. "Well, I don't care for that ugly word. Using it repeatedly shows a distinct lack of vocabulary."

"Give me strength. Once a schoolteacher, always a schoolteacher. I feel a great deal of sympathy for your students."

"My kids just love me. I give them boundaries." She waved her finger at Kat. "And don't think I don't know what you're up to, missy. You're trying to distract me again, and it's not going to happen. We were, as I recall, talking about sex."

"Or the lack thereof," Kat muttered.

"There have been documented surveys that indicate the lack of sex can make a person irritable and/or lethargic or even loud and aggressive. I wouldn't say the last one was you, but you are lethargic and somewhat irritable."

"Documented surveys? In what?" Kat feigned heavy thought. "Let me see. It would have to be the by-product of an article with a title like *How to Please Your Man* for, say, the Testosterone Times. Am I right?"

Em giggled. "Probably was something like that. But, Kat, you do need some human contact. Go out there. Mix. Get some action."

"Not interested, Em. I've had enough of the sort of action you mean."

Em sighed. "I know how hurt you were when Shael called off your relationship, Kat," she said gently. "But you can't just keep dwelling on it. It's not good for you and, well, I worry about you. Just look at yourself. You've lost weight. Too much weight. You're almost catwalk material now."

Kat raised her hands and let them fall. "And that's bad? Some women would kill for a supermodel body. Which is an exaggeration when applied to me, and you know it."

"They might think they'd kill for a string bean body but, you know, real people, and I'm talking men and women, prefer a firm healthy body. That doesn't always mean wraithlike. It depends on your body type. It's in your genes. Now, some people would call me fat, but I just consider myself to be the correct weight for my genetic makeup." Em took a breath.

"Joe wouldn't have it any other way," Kat said quickly, taking advantage of the nanosecond of silence.

"Right. Joe wouldn't want to change me because he loves me. But that's beside the point. Being as thin as you are isn't right for you, Kat. Not health-wise. And that's what's worrying me. You can't be eating properly."

Kat shrugged. "I eat when I'm hungry." She sighed, knowing her jeans were loose on her hips. "Sometimes it's too much trouble to cook for one. And I was never into cooking anyway."

"Then cook for three and freeze the leftovers for another day."

A flash of pain clutched at Kat's heart, and she flinched.

"Oh, Kat." Em reached across and took Kat's hand sympathetically. "I'm sorry, I didn't mean that the way it came out."

"I miss her, Em," Kat said softly.

"I know, love. But I just wish Shael had been deserving of your love."

"Actually, I wasn't thinking about Shael. I guess our relationship was over four years ago, long before she met Tori, when she had that fling—and that's how Shael described it— with her personal trainer. She said it was a moment's lapse in judgment on her part. That it was a once-off. I believed her, because I wanted to believe her. She said it wouldn't happen again, and I gave her another chance. I know I shouldn't have let her sweet talk me into that." Kat shook her head. "But she held the ace back then, Em, and she knew it. She still does—and always will."

Em nodded. "Megghan."

"She was eight months old when Shael and I got together. I've helped raise her. I've been part of her life for ten years, and I couldn't love her more if I'd given birth to her myself. But I didn't. Shael did. That's the bottom line." A tear rolled down Kat's cheek and she dashed it away. "I just miss her so much. Those funny little jokes she loves to tell. The books we read together. It's cut my heart out, Em."

Em stood up and came around the small table. She enveloped Kat in a warm hug, holding her, murmuring soothingly, letting

Kat sob. Eventually Kat pushed away, pulled some tissues from the box on the table. She blew her nose and grimaced.

"Sorry. I just can't seem to lift myself out of this, Em. And I can't even bring Meggie here for a weekend because the place is so horrible." She looked around at the small dingy flat. "And I can't move into a new place until we sort out all our finances and the house." Kat sighed brokenly. "I don't want to force Shael to sell the house either. It's Meggie's home."

"Surely Shael can float you enough cash to get a better flat now. Why in heaven's name did you allow her to put your bank account in her name only."

"I trusted her. I still do in that respect. I know she'll give me my money eventually. She's just playing her control games. Besides, she'll have to hand it over when everything's settled."

Em shook her head. "And until then you have to exist in this place." Em shuddered. "If not Shael, I wish you'd let me help you out."

"Thanks, Em. I appreciate the offer, but I'm not destitute. Not quite, anyway. I've opened a new account for my wages, and I have a bit of cash put aside from my grandmother's estate. It was just that I had to find somewhere to live quickly and the rental market has more demand than supply just now. This was all there was available near work and near Meggie." She gave a rueful laugh. "At least I do get to take Meggie out at the weekend, and we talk on the phone all the time."

"And I suppose the time you spend with Meggie is when it suits Shael?"

"I'll take any time with Meggie I can get."

"How does Meggie feel about all this?" Em asked.

Kat bit her lip. "She thinks it sucks, as she puts it, but she knows things are at a stalemate at the moment."

They sat down again, and Kat topped up their coffee. "I'm just—" She paused. "Concerned. About the custody of Meggie. I don't want Shael to stop me seeing her."

"Would she do that?" Em asked with a frown.

Kat shrugged. "She *is* Meggie's biological mother. She has the final word."

Em muttered derogatorily. "I could use the F-word right about now."

Kat gave a faint smile and Em muttered again.

"I know it's difficult, Kat, but you know that making yourself ill isn't going to help Megghan. Your breakup hasn't been easy on her, and I'd say what she needs at the moment is you, Kat. You healthy and business as usual. Even if it's only for a few hours at a time."

Kat nodded. "I know that, Em. You're right. Maybe you should just tell me it will get easier with time. That's what everyone else tells me," Kat added bitterly.

"I'm not everyone else. I'm Em. I'm like a sister to you. We've known each other since we were five years old."

"I'm sorry, Em. I—" Kat made an appeasing movement with her hand.

"It won't be easy, love. Divorce never is, straight or gay or lesbian. But it's definitely not going to get any easier if you don't want it to. You have to choose to make it so. I'm afraid this is where the dreaded choice comes into play. As I see it, you have two choices here. Keep on wallowing or pull yourself out of it."

A spurt of anger had Kat sitting straighter in her chair, her dark eyes flashing, and Em looked pleased.

"It's such a relief to see you're still in there, love. The real Katrin Oldfield."

Kat laughed mirthlessly. "The real Katrin Oldfield? I'm not sure I know her anymore."

"I remember her. The come-out-fighting Kat who wouldn't give in before the battle begins," Em said passionately. "These past few years I thought I'd lost her."

"And I could ask about the real Mary Margaret Martin?" Kat countered wryly. "I thought you were a lover, not a fighter?"

"I was. I still am but," she shrugged, "needs must, as they say. And at the expense of repeating myself, what you need is some therapeutic loving, otherwise known as meaningless sex. Go out to one of your lesbian venues. Find some willing woman who's looking for the same thing and doesn't mind someone skinny but still sexy and, well, I'll leave the rest to you."

"Em, give it up. I'm not interested in another relationship, meaningless or otherwise. I've had two and stuffed them both up. I'm a bad risk. I can't do relationships apparently."

"Kat! I'm not talking relationship. Surely there are lesbians around who just want an uncomplicated bit of the old X-rated no strings attached."

"X-rated?" Kat repeated. "Meaningless, uncomplicated sex? And what would you know about all that, you good Catholic girl, you? I seem to recall, and correct me if I'm wrong, that you were the one who always advocated no sex before marriage. True or false?"

"It just happens to work for me," Em said defensively. "Why do you think I've been married three times? But you, Kat, are a different matter."

"One of the lucky ones who can have sex before marriage, I take it!" Kat remarked dryly.

"Not what I meant and you know it, missy. I mean that at the moment I think you need something, or someone, to boost your confidence, a shot of adrenaline for your flagging self-esteem, so to speak."

"And sex will do that?" Kat laughed despite herself.

"Absolutely," Em declared with conviction.

"I can't believe I'm hearing this. I'm shocked. Where has the aforementioned good Catholic girl disappeared to?" Kat waved her finger at Em. "You just make sure you mention all this at your next confession, Mary Margaret Martin."

"I'm not talking promiscuous. I'm talking, well, medicinal." Em grinned. "But if it helps you, my best friend, then that one confession will be worth it."

"It should surely give Father David a thrill. Be sure to be particularly graphic."

"Kat! Stop!" Em put her fingers in her ears. "I'm not listening."

Kat chuckled and Em laughed too. She shook her head. "You're a rat, Kat. Father David's coming for dinner Saturday night. How am I going to look him in the face? Because I'm going to be thinking about this, you can be sure."

"I could almost wish I could be there to see it," Kat said, highly amused.

"You can come if you like. For some unknown reason Father David's very fond of you."

"I'm sure he is," Kat remarked dryly. "He's convinced I'm a card-carrying member of Agnostics Anonymous, and it's given him a mission."

"Don't give me that agnostic stuff, Kat. You came to church with me quite often when we were kids. I always felt very pious because I'd collected the most brownie points bringing a Protestant to Mass."

They laughed together and chatted on about the old days.

"What's the name of that cute-looking woman I met at the kids concert last month?" Em asked as Kat refilled their coffee cups.

She frowned. "What concert? Meggie's end-of-term one I dragged you to?"

"Yes. In the Hawaiian segment where Meggie wore that grass skirt. The cute woman's son was standing beside Meggie."

Kat frowned again.

"She had on black jeans and a black tank top. The cute woman, I mean. Nice figure. Muscles, nicely defined. Come-to-bed brown eyes."

"And you tell me you're straight? Sure you haven't come over to the dark side?"

"No. I haven't. And I still can't see what's so bad about hetero sex. Whoever set the design for it in stone had to have had a sense of humor, but all that aside it still feels pretty good."

"And I keep telling you to try a woman and *pretty good* will become *absolutely fantastic.*"

"So you do persist in telling me. And I promise if I do decide to give it a trial run I'll come looking for you. Only you."

"Be still my beating heart!" Kat grimaced. "As great as it would be, I wouldn't be able to cope with the hurt look on Joe's face."

Em threw back her head and laughed. "That makes two of us. So. You stay on the rainbow tracks, and I stay on the straight and apparently narrow."

When they'd stopped laughing, Em picked up the thread of her previous conversation. "But, in the meantime, what about that woman in black?"

Kat shook her head. "You're like a dog with a bone, tenacious to the end."

"So, who is she?" Em persisted. "Do you know her?"

"Billy Carter's mother. Her husband's a sheep shearer."

"Husband? Wow! That's a surprise. She definitely looks like a lesbian. How disappointing."

Kat rolled her eyes.

"But," Em held up her hand, "if her husband's a sheep shearer, he'll be away a lot. She must get lonely so she's a prime candidate for a bit of no-strings-attached sex."

"Em, enough! That's so—so gross!"

Em chuckled. "It is, isn't it? But seriously, Kat, you do need to get out. You can't just hibernate in this awful place." She looked around. "It's depressing."

Kat sighed. "You'll get no argument from me on that score. But I don't have the emotional energy to look for someplace else. It'll have to do till things get sorted out. Then I'll rethink. On the plus side, as I said, it's close to work and Meggie."

Em took a slow sip of her coffee. "There is another option."

"Isn't an option just a smidgen behind a choice?" Kat asked in mock concern.

Em frowned slightly. "Not always. Not in this instance anyway."

Kat threw her hands in the air in mock surrender. "Okay. I know I'm going to regret this—what is your idea of another of my so-called options?"

"Do I detect an edge of sarcasm? Very unbecoming, love. Especially in one so young."

"Young? I'm the same age as you are."

"I know. But I was thinking, what about the house Ruth left you?"

Kat stilled. "You know that subject's taboo. I don't want to talk about that. I think the long-term tenants have just moved out, and the real estate agents have suggested I put the place on the market, sell it as is. Apart from that, the house is older than this unit block."

"Remember years ago," Em continued, undaunted, "before

you met Shael, we were talking about hopes and aspirations. You said you wanted to buy an old house and renovate it. Don't you see, Kat. This is your chance to do just that."

"Em—"

"No, Kat. Hear me out. Eighteen months ago when Ruth left you the house—"

"I never wanted anything from Ruth," Kat put in quickly. *It had been a shock to hear Ruth Dunleavy was dead. Beautiful, exciting, sensual, ruthless Ruth.* "When Ruth and I, well— We made a clean break." Kat gave a mirthless laugh. "What was it you were saying about bad choices? Well, Ruth was my first. First love. First just about everything. Oh, and not forgetting my first major bad choice, too," she added bitterly.

"She cared enough about you to leave you her house when she died," Em said softly.

Kat made no comment.

"Even if it was guilty conscience for the way she treated you," Em continued.

"Ruth was never guilty about anything," Kat sighed. "I'm sure she simply forgot to change her will after we broke up."

"I don't think that's something someone would forget. Ruth had years to change her will regarding you and forgetting holds no water. She left her unit to what was her name? Janelle? Wasn't that her current partner? And there were any number of sweet young things in between you and her. No, Kat, Ruth meant you to have the house for whatever reasons. And it's not as though she had any family to leave her property to. Janelle got her unit, the University got a trust for future scholarships, which was great of her, and she left you her house. Seems fair to me. And, dare I say it of Ruth, very honorable."

Kat remained silent.

"I remember when you told me Ruth had left you the house you said you should sell it because it was the kind of old family home that deserved to have someone give it lots of much-needed TLC."

Kat nodded reluctantly. "That's what I should have done. But I never seemed to have the time to get it all organized. And Shael certainly had no interest in it, apart from making snide remarks about it and Ruth. It was easier at the time to simply leave the tenants in the house and forget it existed."

"What about the rent you've collected?" Em asked.

"Whatever was left after the rates and insurances were paid I gave to charity. It wasn't much anyway because the tenants were old friends of Ruth's, and she only collected a nominal rent."

"Okay," Em went on, "so if you're still set on selling the house, use the school holidays to fix the place up. I came home past there last week when I visited Mum and Dad and from what I saw, it certainly needs some cleaning up. And that way you get away from here, have a change of scene, which you'll admit you need. You have to see you can't spend your entire vacation sitting here alone. Nothing could be worse. Fixing the old house up will give you somewhere to live that isn't this depressingly dingy flat, and the renovating will keep you busy. Then, if you do decide to sell the house, you'll get a much better price for it."

"And all I need to do is move the house to another location. Have you thought about that? It's too complicated, Em. Surely you don't expect I'd be welcomed home?"

"Kat, it was years ago. It's old news. No one will care."

"And my parents? My sister?" Kat shook her head. "You know I haven't spoken to Mum and Dad for over ten years. And I've only very occasionally spoken with Beth."

"Maybe it's time to forgive and forget. Life's short."

"I'm still the daughter with the distasteful lifestyle. Mum and Dad aren't going to change their views on that issue. I don't need to put myself through any of that. Not at the moment. Not on top of everything else."

"Fair enough. But you wouldn't have to see them. It's not like our roots are in a one-horse town. Even suburbia is part of the big city. You know, my mother tells me there are only two families from the old days left in our street."

"So you're saying no one will remember the scandal that swept the township when Ruth and I got together and actual lesbians roamed the streets."

"It was hardly a scandal, Kat. It was a storm in a teacup. And it really wasn't as though the whole town knew."

"Just a select few, do you reckon?" Kat put in.

"Pretty much so."

"That wasn't quite how my mother saw it."

Em pursed her lips. "Rubbish! It was only your own immediate family. Oh, and my parents who got it out of me as usual. But we didn't tell anyone else. And it was very lucky for Ruth that everyone didn't know. She could have lost her job. Come to that, Ruth Dunleavy could have lost her job on more than one occasion. It wasn't just you she took advantage of."

"She didn't take advantage of me. I knew what I was doing, and I was way above the age of consent."

"Not emotionally. Kat, you were eighteen, she was thirty-six. She was a predator."

"And I was in love with her," Kat said softly, her memories flashing up a picture of Ruth the first time she saw her. In a heartbeat she slipped back sixteen years.

It was her first week at University and she was hurrying from one class to another. She'd lost her way and was running late. Racing around a corner of the hallway she'd collided with a warm, firm body. They both landed on the floor in a tangle of arms, legs and books.

When Kat struggled into a sitting position she was facing a stunningly attractive woman. Her jet black hair was pulled into a severe chignon that emphasized the clean lines of her classic features. But it was her eyes that held Kat mesmerized—liquid brown fringed by long dark lashes, and they were deep and full of a terrifying, forbidden promise.

The brown eyes took time to slowly study Kat's face, moved downwards over her breasts and her jean-clad legs before returning to Kat's face and Kat blushed. Those knowing, incredible eyes didn't miss Kat's discomfort as she shifted self-consciously. What would this incredibly attractive woman see when she looked at Kat, she wondered. Ordinary brown hair and eyes and an unremarkable face.

"I'm really sorry," she got out, wanting the floor to open up and swallow her.

The woman stood up with one lithe movement, and her tailored skirt moved upwards to show a tantalizing expanse of smooth, silk-clad thigh. She held out her hand and pulled Kat to her feet.

Kat wanted to lean closer, but she made herself step backwards and she apologized again.

The woman laughed, slowly smoothed her skirt and her fitted jacket. "It takes two to tango," she said, her voice husky and to Kat's ears, incredibly sexy. "It was as much my fault. No harm done, except to our dignities."

Kat stood staring and then hurriedly retrieved the woman's books before gathering her own. The woman glanced at the title of the book on top of Kat's pile and raised her eyebrows slightly before giving Kat that small intimate smile, the smile Kat later realized was Ruth's trademark. She moved, and Kat stepped aside to give her space. Even so Kat felt the brush of the smooth fabric of her jacket on her bare arm. Her skin tingled as she flushed again.

"I'll see you around, hmmm?" said the woman, her husky tone a terrifying caress.

Even her embarrassment couldn't prevent Kat from watching the woman as she walked down the hallway. There was a whole story in the way she moved, held herself, and a wave of envy joined the rush of raging hormones. How Kat wished she had that self-confidence, that grace, that exciting aura of sensual promise.

Of course the woman was a little older than Kat, she told herself placatingly, so she wouldn't be floundering around in an agony of finding her way in what was the totally new and unchartered environment of the University. Although Kat loved the old buildings, the green lawns, the wonderful old trees and the stream of students, she knew she'd led a relatively sheltered life. The world was opening up to her, and it was only natural that she would be a little off center until she was used to all these changes.

And her attraction to the woman was all part of the newness of her growing suspicion that she wasn't the same as her best friend, Em, and the rest of the young women she knew. She couldn't bring herself to tell even Em that she thought she was a lesbian because she wasn't really sure herself.

Maybe it was simply a case of her not having met the right man, she thought as she hurried along to her class, only to pause again as the woman's arresting face swam in her mind. She swallowed as her mouth went dry and a spiral of awareness clutched at the pit of her stomach and traveled south. Hormones, she told herself as she picked up her pace. She'd only been talking to Em about hormones the evening before. Of course, Em had been talking about men, specifically a guy in her first class, and Kat was pretty sure anything remotely like lesbianism hadn't crossed Em's mind. But it had crossed Kat's mind.

She lay awake thinking and worrying about it, wondering why she had no feelings, no spark of awareness with Em. Em was her best friend and always had been and Kat loved her dearly. If she was going to be attracted to a girl, why not Em, with her voluptuous figure, her unruly dark curls, her dancing blue eyes and her wonderful smile.

Maybe she wasn't a lesbian after all. When the right guy came along her life would fall into place.

As Kat slid quietly into her seat for her lecture, trying to be invisible, she had a sinking feeling after her encounter in the hallway that the *right man* just wasn't going to do it for her. And she made herself concentrate on her tutor. That turned out to be well-nigh impossible and after a while she gave up, her thoughts rushing back to the intriguing woman in the hallway.

Of course, hurrying into her next lecture, taking a seat next to Em, only to find that same stunning woman from her encounter in the hallway at the front of the class and introducing herself as Professor Ruth Dunleavy, had done absolutely nothing to restore Kat's equilibrium.

The woman was a professor? Kat's heart sank as she cringed with embarrassment. She'd been so way off the mark thinking the attractive woman was a slightly older student. She'd even allowed herself a delicious moment thinking she might even seek the woman out, get to know her. In her daydream the two had discovered they were both lesbians. She hadn't quite nutted out how this miraculous discovery was to come about, but the end result had had her feeling very hot and she'd squirmed in her seat.

Seeing the woman at the podium in front of their class, half glasses on her beautiful nose as she studied her notes, shot Kat's fantasies down in a kaleidoscope of heartbreaking color. As Kat sat there feeling almost catatonic, Ruth Dunleavy had removed her glasses and run her gaze over her newest students. Her fine dark brows had arched slightly when her gaze settled on Kat. Kat blushed to the roots of her hair as the corners of Ruth's lips lifted in that same secret, knowing smile.

After class Ruth sought Kat out and within a few short weeks they were lovers. Could it really have been sixteen years ago? It seemed like yesterday.

"Earth to Kat!"

Em's voice filtered into Kat's mind bringing Kat back to the present.

"Good grief, Kat. It's so frustrating when you do that."

"Do what?"

"Go off into your own personal wild blue yonder. You're always doing that."

"No I'm not."

"You know you totally freaked me out the first time you did it. We were five years old, and I thought you'd opted to fly up to heaven."

Kat laughed. "And I reckon that was the first time I saw Em the Drama Queen."

Em laughed too. "The Dreamer and the Drama Queen. What a pair. So, what about my idea? About the house?"

"I don't know, Em. I don't think I'm up to it."

"Rubbish! You can do anything. You always have been able to. Heaven only knows why you won't let yourself believe in yourself."

Kat shook her head.

"And if you need ready money I can give you a loan."

"It's not the money, Em. But thanks anyway."

"So, we've more than established it's not the money, but you're still existing here in this dingy dive." Em gave Kat's flat a dismissive wave of her hand. "Why, one may ask?" When Kat didn't comment Em sighed loudly. "I have a theory about all this." She waved her hand again. "All I'll say is you have nothing to punish yourself for."

"Punish myself for? What on earth are you talking about now, Em?"

Em held Kat's gaze and said nothing.

Kat stood up, stepped to the sink, her back to her friend. After a moment she turned back to face her. "Do you really think I'm doing that, Em? Punishing myself?" She looked around the dark, tiny flat. Could Em be right? Kat knew she felt guilty. Shael was an expert at making Kat feel bad. If Kat had been more attentive this wouldn't have happened. If Kat hadn't been so wrapped up in her job she wouldn't have been too tired to go out and party, and Shael wouldn't have needed to look elsewhere. And the list went on.

Had she carried that particular baggage with her? Surely not. She knew none of it was true. It was ridiculous, wasn't it? She glanced back at Em and sighed. "I suspect you might be right," she said softly.

Hadn't Kat hated the flat the moment the real estate agent had shown it to her? And she could have found something better further afield. Yet she'd settled on this awful place, telling herself it was so convenient.

So what was she going to do about it? As Em said, there was Ruth's house. Although she hadn't said anything to Em, she'd been thinking about the house since she finished school last week. The tenants had left two weeks ago, and the agent had been pressing her to re-let it or put it on the market. The agent had said he had half a dozen or more interested parties. Yet Kat had held back, unwilling to make a decision.

"You know if I do this super-woman-renovating thing I'll be tied up twenty-four-seven, and you'll have to come visit me?" Kat heard herself saying before she was aware she'd even decided. "That will be an extra forty-five minute drive."

A huge smile lit Em's face. "It will be so worth it, love. You'll see."

Two days later Kat's car was packed to the roofline, and she was heading for the freeway that would take her to the other side of the city.

CHAPTER TWO

Kat struggled to get the last piece of old carpet into the rubbish skip. She stood back and stretched her back before trudging up the stairs to the house. She paused in the doorway of the living room and admired the timber floor she'd uncovered. It was amazing. When the renovation was finished and the wonderful old wood was sanded and polished it would be magnificent.

In fact, the whole place was magnificent and oozing potential. Kat had climbed the steps that first afternoon, put the key in the lock and opened the door to a new chapter of her life. Even then the house had had a welcoming feel, as though it had been waiting for her. And more than once in the few days she'd been here it had occurred to her that perhaps this choice, or as Em put it, this particular direction at the fork in the highway of her life might be the right one for a change.

Back when Kat was with Ruth she'd never been inside this house because it had always been rented out. Ruth had an elegant unit near the University with views over the Brisbane River. The unit was straight out of a *Beautiful Living* magazine, all state-of-the-art appliances Ruth rarely used, and expensive, aesthetic furniture.

They'd been together for months before they realized they were from the same Brisbane suburb. In fact, their families lived only half a dozen streets apart. Ruth's parents had died a few years earlier and on their one visit back together, a visit with disastrous results, they'd only driven past the house where Ruth had grown up. Ruth had told Kat friends of hers were renting the place. Until the solicitors had contacted Kat after Ruth died she hadn't known that Ruth still owned the place.

It was a large house, considering Ruth had been an only child and having the verandas built in had made it even bigger. Ruth had explained that her parents had both been academics and each had needed a large study. Hence the built-in verandas. My humble beginnings, Ruth had laughingly called it, and Kat could remember wondering how this ordinary family home could have produced such a beautiful, exotic creature.

Yet it had. Ruth had been both exotic and beautiful.

Kat sighed. Ruth Dunleavy had certainly been Kat's first major bad decision. However, looking back from the present to that part of her life wasn't something Kat allowed herself to do very often. In the beginning it had been far too painful and as the pain passed a jumbled mixture of hurt, regret and sadness had taken over. If anyone had asked her that age-old question about having your life to live over again and whether or not you would change it, Kat suspected her reply had mellowed somewhat.

In the beginning it had been all about wishing she'd never met Ruth. Now it was probably more about regret that Ruth had let not only Kat down, but herself, with her less than honorable behavior. Kat grimaced. Now who was being sanctimonious, she asked herself.

But would she have changed things so that she hadn't met

Ruth? Kat knew she wouldn't have. Ruth had been good for Kat in so many ways. With her self-confidence. With what Kat perceived as her slow transition to adulthood. She'd always seen herself as years behind her peers emotionally, and if there was such a word, world-wisely. Kat grinned to herself. With Ruth's encouragement, Kat had blossomed. Kat had needed someone like Ruth at that time in her life.

Perhaps Ruth hadn't really been the right person, but she'd certainly been in the right place at the right time. Ruth had been the one to draw Kat out into the place she needed to be, had made her face the truth she'd been hiding for years. Ruth had saved her from taking the path that had been set out for her, the path everyone expected her to follow.

If Em was right about forks in the road of life, then Ruth had taken Kat along a different fork, the one that led away from what was considered to be the conventional one. Kat sighed again. It wasn't that she didn't want the house with the picket fence, kids and a dog running around the garden. She'd just wanted to share it with a woman.

Kat's first step, although terrifying at first, had been in the right direction. She'd just chosen the wrong person to travel with.

Yet it had seemed so right. Kat had been so absolutely besotted by Ruth she'd hated having to keep their relationship so secret. She'd wanted the world to know. And she'd wanted her family to know Ruth. At first Ruth had flatly refused to meet Kat's family but Kat had persisted, and she'd eventually agreed to meet them. If Ruth's parents had been alive Kat would have wanted to meet them, she assured Ruth. Ruth had given her an exasperated look and agreed that her parents would have loved Kat. Then she'd held up her hand and said enough was enough. She'd do the quick hello and then she was off.

Kat had been ecstatic over the compromise. Ruth would drive Kat to the house, meet Kat's parents, and then go off to visit friends, leaving Kat to socialize with her family. At that stage Kat would have agreed to anything to be part of Ruth's life and have her family know Ruth was part of her life.

Kat drifted back and saw herself that tumultuous afternoon

in Ruth's restored MG sports car, the wind catching wayward strands of her dark hair, her hand resting on Ruth's leg. They were going to see Kat's parents at last.

The only cloud in the clear blue of Kat's sky had been Ruth's reluctance to want to meet Kat's parents. However, she was going to meet them and, no matter how brief the visit, her parents would know Kat was making wonderful friends.

Ruth had driven past her childhood home, not far from where Kat had grown up. Kat in turn showed Ruth where Em's family lived and then they were pulling up in front of the Oldfield home. It looked sturdy and tidy, having only been painted a few months earlier. Kat's father kept the lawns mowed and the garden edges trimmed but as her mother didn't care for flowers there was no color in the garden.

Kat led Ruth up the path and she rang the bell and called through the open door. "Mum. Dad. It's Kat."

Ann Oldfield came to the door and unlocked the security screen. "You didn't call to say you were coming, Katrin," her mother said.

"It was a spur-of-the-moment thing. I was in the neighborhood and, well, I wanted to introduce you and Dad to a friend. Is Dad home?" Kat wished her mother would look just a little pleased to see her. "Can we come in?"

Her mother stood back and Kat stepped into the living room. Only then did her mother catch sight of Ruth as she prepared to follow Kat inside. If anything, her mother's frown deepened. At that moment Kat's father joined them from the kitchen.

"Dad. Hello. I'm glad you're here too."

"It's Saturday afternoon, Katrin," her mother remarked. "Where else would your father be?"

"You just missed Beth," her father said and stopped when his wife frowned at him.

Kat swallowed. Her parents seemed impossibly more sober and distant than they usually were and she suddenly wondered why she'd wanted to bring Ruth to meet them at all. She should have taken Ruth to meet Em's parents. Sometimes she felt closer to the Martins than she did her own family. "Ah, Mum. Dad. I wanted you to meet a friend of mine. From University. In fact, she's one of my tutors. This is Ruth Dunleavy. And Ruth, meet my parents, John and Ann Oldfield."

Ruth took off her sunglasses. "Nice to meet you. Kat talks so much about you."

Not exactly the truth, Kat reflected.

Her parents remained silent and Kat tensed. "Ruth's family used to live a few streets over. Near the park."

"We know where she lived and we know who she is," Kat's mother said, "and we don't want her in our home."

Kat drew a sharp breath, slid a horrified glance at Ruth. "Mum. I don't know—"

"It's all over the village. And I don't know how you can show your face here with her."

"Mum, what are talking about?" A glimmer of disquiet made Kat pause. Could her mother have found out about her relationship with Ruth? Surely not? Kat had had no intention of coming out to her parents just yet. She'd wanted them to get to know Ruth first. Apart from that, how would her mother have found out anyway? Ruth always insisted they be discreet. Kat had only just told Em, and Em wouldn't have told Kat's parents. Would she? Kat swallowed, feeling a blush begin to color her cheeks. "What village?" she asked inanely.

"Here," said her mother sharply, pointing at the worn carpet of the living room. "Where we live. Where your father and I have lived for forty years. And now you do this to us. We can't look the neighbors in the face. I can't even go to the shops."

Kat slid another glance at Ruth, absolutely mortified Ruth had to see and hear her mother like this, but Ruth looked more amused than annoyed. Kat held up her hand. "Mum, stop!"

"I won't stop. And I'm not having the likes of you telling me what to do. After all we've done for you." Her mother shook her head.

"Ann," Kat's father began, but his wife silenced him with a look.

"How could you do this to us, Katrin?" her mother asked.

"Do what, Mum?"

"Behave in this abhorrent way, that's what." Ann Oldfield glared at Ruth. "And you, you're old enough to know better.

How dare you take advantage of our daughter, lead her astray?"

"Mum! Ruth hasn't done anything of the kind." Kat shook her head, growing agitated. It was worse than she'd thought.

"She must have. You aren't one of those people, Katrin. She must have put the idea in your mind."

"Mum. It wasn't, it isn't, like that. Please let me explain—"

"You don't need to explain. It's that...that woman," Kat's mother jabbed her finger towards Ruth. "She's the one who should be explaining. And I'm telling you now—Katrin's father and I are not having it. We'll go to the police."

Kat stared at her mother in disbelief. "Mum, I'm eighteen years old. And it's my life. You can't dictate who I can or can't be friends with."

"Friends! We know you and that woman are more than friends." She gave a disgusted exclamation.

"Who told you all this?" Kat asked, angry now.

"Everyone down at your father's club knew about it. And we were oblivious. You made us look like fools. Until someone took pity on us and told us you were living with a known—" her mother paused. "Lesbian," she bit out. "Everyone knows what she is."

"Mum, Ruth and I are just—"

"Your daughter's a wonderful young woman, Mrs. Oldfield." Ruth spoke for the first time. "She's attractive, bright and she's a lesbian. If you love her you'll accept her for who she is."

"They're fine words, Miss University Professor, but I don't want people talking about my daughter the way they talk about you."

Kat looked at Ruth and only the two spots of color on her cheeks gave any indication she was upset.

"What exactly are they saying?" Ruth asked tersely.

"Ruth, don't." Kat put her hand on Ruth's arm. "Please. Let's go."

But Ruth stood her ground.

"No. Your mother's making wild accusations. I think we should ask her what she thinks people are saying." She turned back to Kat's mother. "I'd like to hear it and, please, be specific," she finished acidly.

"That you're a lesbian. That you prey on young women, young women like Katrin, turn them into lesbians, that your morals are no better than an alley cat, that you act like a man and that your behavior killed your parents."

"I see. Well, most of the first bit is certainly true although I dispute your terminology. I can't deny I'm a lesbian, but I don't go around trying to convert people. Why would I need to? There are plenty of lesbians around." She paused to smile at Kat. "Like your daughter."

"Mum, Ruth didn't turn me into a lesbian. I knew I was different. Ruth just showed me why I felt that way."

"Your daughter had a choice." Ruth shrugged. "She chose me."

Kat's mother's lips pursed. "You're no better than—"

Ruth gave a sharp laugh. "Ah, my morals again. If I was a man no one would turn a hair. Isn't that so? I'd simply be playing the field, sowing my wild oats. Isn't that what they used to call it?"

"You broke your mother's heart," Ann Oldfield repeated.

"My mother, both my parents, knew I was a lesbian and they supported me. It's a pity you can't do the same for your own daughter."

They all stood silently for long moments.

"However," said Ruth almost chattily, "look on the bright side. At least I'm not going to get her pregnant."

The color seemed to drain from Kat's parents' faces. Her mother recovered first. "You're an evil, abhorrent person. Get out of our house!" She turned back to face Kat. "And if you continue to associate with this…this person, Katrin, then you can leave with her."

"Mum, please! Dad? I'm a lesbian. I can't change who I am. Can't you see that?" Kat swallowed tears.

"You can choose not to live such a horrible lifestyle. And until you come to your senses, you're not welcome here."

"Ann." Kat's father stepped forward, but her mother took hold of his arm.

"No, John. What she's doing is unchristian. It's an abomination against all we've brought her up to be, all the standards we've set for her. Until she sees the error of her ways I don't want her here." She turned and gave Ruth another hate-filled look before facing Kat again. "Get out, Katrin. And take this woman with you. Your father and I don't want her here."

Kat drew herself up to her full height as she met and held her mother's gaze. "I can't change, Mum, and if you can't accept that and accept Ruth, then I'm going and I'm not coming back."

"That's your choice," her mother said and turned and went into the kitchen.

"Dad?" Kat appealed to her father, but he just looked away, not making a comment.

After that, Kat never went back. Neither had her parents tried to contact her. Kat had spoken to her sister intermittently over the years, but Beth had made no comment on the situation between Kat and their parents. Until that afternoon, Kat hadn't known how homophobic her parents were. Her family weren't regular church goers so it hadn't occurred to Kat that her mother would use Christian morals against her. At the time, with her emotions raw, she was convinced they saw the whole thing as a justifiable reason to be rid of her.

Kat turned and looked at the front room. If she removed all the lining and cladding, the veranda could live again, bringing the house back to its former glory, a gracious old Queenslander in keeping with a lot of earlier houses in the suburb.

But could Kat do it? Was she physically up to tearing down walls? Well, she'd torn up carpet without much trouble. How hard could the walls be? She eyed her trusty hammer and jimmy bar.

She crossed and ran her hand over the smooth surface of the lining. Could it be the dreadful asbestos sheeting so prevalent in old buildings that could be so life threatening? Before she touched it she knew she'd have to get professional advice. But who?

Kat went back into the living room and rummaged around on one of the two upturned packing cases that along with the single folding chair and the inflatable bed made up the only furnishings. Where was that card Grace had given her?

Grace Worrall and her husband Tom lived next door. Two days after Kat arrived Grace came through the side gate to introduce herself. She'd brought over homemade pikelets smothered in strawberry jam and cream and Kat had made tea. The Worralls had been neighbors of the Dunleavys for more than thirty years and Grace and Ruth had been friends. Grace was a couple of years older than Ruth and had been married for less than a year when the Worralls moved in while Ruth was attending University.

"I had two children fairly quickly, and I felt a little tied down, what with Tom working such long hours." Grace told Kat. "Ruth saved my sanity more than once, I can tell you."

Kat noticed a fleeting softness in Grace's expression before Grace changed the subject to ask Kat about her job, her life. But that look did make Kat wonder if Ruth and Grace had been more than friends. No. She was imagining the look in Grace's eyes and reminded herself Grace was married. Like that meant anything to the Ruth Kat had known. Hadn't she caught Ruth in the proverbial compromising position with a fellow professor's young wife?

Then Grace was asking Kat what she had in mind for the house.

Until she arrived Kat had intended to simply make minor repairs, give the house a fresh coat of paint and then sell it. But standing in the old house and listening to its distinctive subtle sounds gave her a glow of excitement. She now knew each nuance of soft sound—the old corrugated iron roof expanding and contracting with the changing temperature, the one creaky floorboard in the hallway, the slither of the old silky oak timber sash windows as she raised and lowered them. And she knew this place, this change of scene, had been the reason the dark fog lifted, the fog that had descended on her when she'd known her relationship with Shael was over.

With a rush of enthusiasm she'd given Grace Worrall a rough idea of her plans, plans she hadn't been conscious she'd made. A new bathroom and kitchen. Adding an en suite and walk-in wardrobe to the back bedroom. Painting. Polishing the floors.

Grace was amazed. "You're not going to do it all yourself, are you? I mean, that's a lot of work."

Kat grimaced. "No, I'm not that confident in my carpentry abilities. I plan on doing the rough work, but bathrooms and kitchens are jobs for the professionals, I think. I just have to arrange to get some quotes."

"Oh, good. And have you anyone in mind? For the quotes, I mean."

"Not yet. I guess I'll just consult the Yellow Pages or the local newspaper." Kat hadn't quite got that far.

"Then I hope you won't think me meddling, but I can recommend my nephew's firm," Grace said. "My brother started the business but he's retired recently, so his son and his wife and her cousin run it now. I'll bring over one of their cards later. They're exceptionally good and reasonably priced, too."

Grace had dutifully returned later with the card Kat now held in her hand. *Handy Andrews & Son. Renovations and Repairs.* That about covered it, Kat thought. *No job too big or too small. Reasonable prices.* Mmm, reasonable prices. Kat pulled a face. That was imperative because she was on a tight budget. *Ring for a free quote.*

Kat picked up the phone from the floor and three hours later as she sat on the front steps sipping a welcome cup of tea, a tidy van pulled to the curb in front of the house. On the side of the van was a cartoon character of a builder holding a hammer in one hand and a paint roller in the other. *HANDY ANDREWS* was written in bold, bright letters along with the phone number.

The van door opened and a booted foot appeared followed by a head of short streaky blond hair. Next came a trim body clad in light khaki tailored shorts and a matching short-sleeved khaki work shirt. For a moment Kat thought it was a slim youth. Then the figure turned, and it was obvious this was a nicely curved female.

CHAPTER THREE

Kat stood up and caught the woman's eye. She waved and smiled before turning back to her van. She leaned over and reached inside, emerging with a small briefcase in her hand.

Not that Kat registered that just then. She was still taking herself to task for noticing the way the woman's shorts hugged her nicely rounded backside. Which anyone would have glanced at, Kat told herself, watching the woman cross the footpath to the gate. The woman's body was perfectly proportioned, neither too thin nor too fat, and her short straight hair gleamed in the sunlight.

She continued up the path and stopped, one booted foot on the bottom step, hand on the railing. "Katrin Oldfield, I presume?" she asked, still smiling. Her voice had an underlying huskiness that was full of vitality and so fascinating.

Her bright, friendly smile drew the same from Kat. It seemed so long since Kat had smiled spontaneously that her facial muscles felt stiff and unresponsive. Apart from that, now that the woman was closer, Kat could see just how attractive she was. Perhaps she wasn't beautiful in the accepted sense of the word, but her wide friendly smile, bright eyes, the curve of her jaw and her determined chin, made her quite arresting.

Kat swallowed, annoyed with herself that she was even letting her thoughts head in that direction. She reminded herself again that she wasn't interested in any relationship. She'd been there, done that—she was in emotional overload.

And the warning bells went off when she noticed the sun glint on the ring on the woman's left hand. It was a definite no-go area, she told herself. No way was Kat getting anywhere near a straight woman. But she could appreciate the woman's good looks, couldn't she?

She gave an embarrassed cough. "Yes, I'm Kat Oldfield."

The woman continued up the stairs and Kat, mug in hand, moved backwards so the woman could step into the sleep-out. Now, standing on the same level together, Kate could see the woman was far more petite than she had realised. And close up she was even more attractive. Her skin had a healthy outdoorsy glow and her smile, well, Kat felt she could just sit watching that smile forever.

"Hi, Kat." The woman held out her hand. "I'm Jess Andrews from Handy Andrews. You rang this morning for a quote, I believe."

"Yes. That's right." Kat pulled herself together with no little effort and shook Jess Andrews' outstretched hand. "I'm impressed that you could get out here so soon."

"We try to follow up as quickly as we can. There's nothing more frustrating I always think when you want a quote yesterday, and we don't put in an appearance for a week or two." Jess Andrews looked back at the almost full rubbish skip and smiled again. "And I see you've made a start on the renovations."

Kat nodded. "Come on in." They walked into the bare living

room. "Would you like a cup of tea or coffee? I've just boiled the kettle."

"That'd be great. I've been run off my feet today. A cup of tea would hit the spot. Black, one sugar, thanks."

Kat led Jess into the kitchen and set about making the tea while Jess looked around.

"Great place. Stacks of potential, especially this flooring you've uncovered. It's wonderful," she said as Kat handed her a mug of tea. Jess took a sip and murmured her appreciation. "So what do you have in mind for the place?"

"Well, before we get started, I should tell you I'm sort of restricted by my budget."

Jess chuckled. "I know what you mean. I've been told I have champagne tastes on a beer pocket."

Kat couldn't seem to draw her eyes from Jess's lips. She took a quick sip of her tea. "It's something like that with me, too. So I thought perhaps, if you don't mind, we could break the quote up into a couple of stages."

"Sure. That's no problem."

"Firstly, there's the kitchen." She motioned to the Eighties-style kitchen. "And the bathroom's about the same vintage. Then I'd like to turn the back bedroom into the main one. I thought I'd add an extra bathroom off the bedroom, make it into an en suite, with a walk-in wardrobe beside it. And," Kat pulled a face, "I'd like to open up the front and half of the side veranda again, make the house more in keeping with its original style."

"Wow! That would be fantastic," Jess agreed. "It appears to be a good solid building so I see no problem." She grinned. "Apart from said costs."

"Do you think it's financially viable?"

"Of course. And there are ways we can keep the costs down." Jess looked back into the living room. "I can see you've pulled up the carpets. Have you done that on your own? I mean, do you have someone to help you?" Her smile faltered a little, and she brushed a strand of her fair hair back behind her ear.

Was that an innocent question? Kat wondered. Or was it a subtle way for Jess to find out if Kat was single? Oh, for heaven's sake, she chastised herself. That would be stretching it, even for a lovesick teenager, and it was a long time since Kat had been that. And let's not forget the wedding ring on Jess's finger, she reminded herself. But Jess was still waiting for Kat's reply.

"Ah, yes. Just me," she said quickly. "I'm slow but thorough." She grimaced derisively and Jess laughed.

"That's an admirable quality because if you're at all able, you can do some of the ground work yourself and that will save you some cash."

"Music to my ears," Kat put in with a smile.

Jess drained her tea mug and put it in the sink. She set her briefcase on the bench and drew out a clipboard already bearing Kat's details. "Shall we start here in the kitchen?"

Kat nodded. "I don't want anything too fancy. Maybe just some modernizing."

"Okay. So why don't you tell me what you have in mind, and I'll make any suggestions which, of course, you're under no obligation to take any notice of." She laughed again, the husky sound sending a ripple of attraction that teased the pit of Kat's stomach.

Once again Kat couldn't seem to drag her gaze from Jess's lips. Those lips... What if Kat made a few suggestions of her own? Suggestions involving those gorgeous lips? Kat made herself breathe evenly. "I don't have much of an idea about the specifics. Just relatively plain and functional."

"Well, the layout's fairly functional as it is. If you're happy with this setup, I wouldn't suggest moving any of the plumbing because that can get expensive. There's precious little cupboard and bench space, but you can get more compact sinks these days that would help considerably with the extra bench tops. Then maybe new tap-ware as they're very tired and a little dated. And you'd be amazed what new doors on the kitchen cabinets would do. We use a very good kitchen firm called K and T Cabinets. It's a well-established, family-owned business, and they do exceptionally good work for a very reasonable price." She took a color brochure from her briefcase and handed it to Kat. "We sort out what's needed, and they come out and measure it up and then make and install it. On the plus side the oven and cooktop look okay though."

"I think they're only a few years old. The house has been

rented for years to very good, responsible tenants," Kat told her, admiring the photographs of the modern kitchens in the brochure.

"That was lucky. I could tell you some horror stories about tenants. We quite often see the results of bad renters. But Betty and Tess were lovely people."

"You knew them?" Kat asked carefully, glancing up from the brochure.

"Sure. I've known them for years. From visiting Grace and Tom next door. Betty and Tess were good friends of Grace's. Almost part of the family." Jess leaned back against the cupboard unit and crossed one booted foot over the other. "They weren't getting any younger they told Grace, and the yard was becoming too much for Betty to look after. So they decided the time was right to move into a retirement village over at Carseldine." Kat watched as Jess Andrews fiddled with her clipboard. "They were close friends of Ruth's, and I know they were devastated when she was killed in the road accident."

"Yes. It was a shock," Kat said softly.

"Grace said you inherited the house with the stipulation that Betty and Tess could stay here as long as they wanted." Jess paused. "You were a friend of Ruth's too?" she asked casually.

"Yes. Good friends. From University," Kat added with equal casualness.

Jess nodded and unclipped the tape measure from her belt. "Well, let's take some measurements. Want to hold the end of the tape?"

Kat set down her now empty mug and moved forward to hold the tape where Jess indicated.

When they'd finished Jess stood back and gave the kitchen a thoughtful look over.

Kat stood back and surreptitiously studied Jess. Definitely cute. Way, way too cute. Kat paused. Had Jess known that Ruth and her friends, Betty and Tess, were lesbians? In all probability she had. And it wouldn't take much for her to make the jump to the possibility that Kat was a lesbian, too.

As if any of that mattered, Kat told herself. Business was business so what relevance did who Kat slept with have on the situation? Especially to an obviously straight woman. Unless it was against her religious code to deal with people with so-called abhorrent lifestyles. Yet Kat had seen no semblance of that when Jess had mentioned the house's last tenants.

"My only suggestion would be that you lower the height of the shelf for the microwave." Jess's voice brought Kat out of her speculation. Jess flashed Kat another of her attractive smiles. "As one of the vertically challenged I find microwaves are nearly always far too high for me, and I see that as downright dangerous, what with the hot food, etc."

"I see your point," Kat agreed. "I'm five-six and it's too high for me." She ran her eyes over the length of Jess's trim body. When she realized Jess was watching her she flushed.

"I'm five-two," Jess said with a laugh, and she turned back to the kitchen. "Now what about the floor?"

They discussed floor coverings, tap fittings, cupboard door styles and bench tops before moving to the bathroom. Jess efficiently sketched and measured and took notes. When they'd finished Kat led Jess to the back of the house to the third bedroom. It was as large as the front bedroom, and Kat explained her ideas about the extra bathroom and walk-in closet.

"I want to make this bedroom the main one because there's room to add the en suite and wardrobe into what's now the side sleep-out."

"Let's have a look."

They went out onto what used to be an open-sided veranda.

"There's plenty of space for what you want," Jess said thoughtfully. "And you were thinking the rest as open veranda, right?"

Kat nodded. "I want to open out this section and the whole front of the house, but I thought I'd check for asbestos sheeting before I started knocking out the lining here."

"Good thinking." Jess tapped lightly on the wall and ran her hand over the surface. "I'm pretty sure it's safe enough. It's not fibro, but I'd feel better getting Lucas's opinion." She turned back to Kat. "Lucas is my cousin and owns part of Handy Andrews. I'll ask him to drop by tomorrow if you like?"

"I'd appreciate that."

"And I noticed in the living room the ceiling appears to have been lowered." They walked back into the middle of the house. "See." She pointed out the height of the ceiling in the living room compared to the ceiling in the adjoining bedroom. "The living room ceiling should be the same. Houses of this vintage had high ceilings. I'll get Lucas to check in the roof cavity because quite probably you'll have a pressed metal ceiling under there. Have you seen the patterned metal sheet ceilings?"

"I think I have, in a neighbor's house when I was young."

Jess nodded. "Costs the earth to install now so let's keep our fingers crossed."

As Jess checked her paperwork Kat watched her, admiring the soft curve of her cheek.

"This has the most amazing potential—" Jess paused as Kat's mobile phone rang. She excused herself and dug the phone out of her pocket. She glanced at the number displayed and felt herself start to smile. "Hello."

"Hi, Kitty Kat. How are you?" said a young voice. "It's me. Meggie."

Kat's smile widened. "I know. Hi there, sweetie. How could I forget your voice? But this is a surprise. I wasn't expecting you to call." She glanced at her wristwatch. Megghan should be at school. Was she sick? "Are you okay?"

Megghan laughed. "I'm fine. And I just know you're wondering why I'm not at school. Well, it's our form's free day as this is our last week of school. But, you know, if I went to your school I'd be already finished just like you."

Kat grimaced slightly. That had been the source of much complaint from Meggie, and she took every opportunity to mention the fact. She'd wanted to attend the private co-ed school where Kat taught, but her mother had wanted her to go to an all-girls school.

"Give that one up, Megs, you know there's not much chance of changing that."

"I know, Kat." She gave a long suffering sigh. "Mum can be mega stubborn, and I know I just have to live with it. But it sucks. And speaking of Mum, I know your next question is going to be have I asked Mum if I can ring you."

"And have you?" Kat asked.

"Um, well, no. But I will tell her I've rung when she gets home."

"When she gets home? Isn't she there?"

"She's working. But Tori's here. She's asleep. So I thought, well, I'd just ring. I really wanted to talk, Kat. You don't mind me ringing you, do you?" She asked, and Kat's heart ached at the underlying vulnerability in her tone.

"Of course I don't mind. You know you can ring me anytime. Day or night."

"I miss you, Kat."

Kat's shoulders sagged. "I miss you, too, love."

"Can I come and see you? I could get the train or a bus. I've looked up the schedules myself on the net, and I'm sure Mum would let me if she knows you'd pick me up at the station."

"I don't think that's a good idea, Megs. I'll come and get you."

"But when? I really do miss you, Kat. It's no fun here without you, and we've just started watching the tenth season of *Stargate SG-1*. We're way behind." Her voice broke and Kat clutched the phone.

"Don't cry, love."

"Sorry, Kat. I just miss you." Megghan sniffed loudly. "Have you been working on the old house?" she asked bravely.

"Yes. From dawn to dusk."

"I can help, you know. I could come and stay and help you. We finish school on Friday and I'll have nothing to do. I know you have no furniture, but I can bring my sleeping bag and I can sleep on the floor."

Kat laughed. "No need for that. I have a blow-up bed now. And I have a little machine to inflate it."

Megghan laughed. "I want to see it, Kat. When can I? This weekend?"

"Megs, you know that's not up to me," Kat began.

"I know. Mum." Megghan paused. "There's Mum's car now. She's home. Can you ring her later and ask her if I can come over? Give her time to unwind and then ring. Will you, Kat?"

Kat sighed. "Okay. I'll ring later. In the meantime, don't worry. We'll work something out."

"Promise?"

"I promise."

"I love you, Kat."

"I love you, too, Megs."

"I have to go now. Mum's coming. 'Bye, Kat."

"'Bye, love." Kat hung up and stood looking at the phone in her hand.

The situation was intolerable, and the worst thing about it was it was out of Kat's control. Shael held all the aces. Kat expelled the breath she was holding as a sound behind her brought her back to the present.

Jess Andrews was taking more measurements and had dropped her clipboard. She bent to retrieve it and slid a quick glance at Kat. "I guess that about does it. What's the best time for Lucas to call over tomorrow to check the paneling?"

"Any time. Whatever suits you."

Jess smiled. "He'll probably make it early if that's okay?"

"Sure."

They stood in silence for long moments before Jess crossed towards Kat. Kat took a step back and then felt foolish as Jess reached out for her briefcase.

"I'll do a rough estimate that won't include hardware because that will depend on the units you choose. But it will give you some idea of the cost. And I'll break it down into sections. Kitchen. Bathroom. En suite and robe. Okay?"

"That would be great."

Jess held out her hand and Kat took hold of it. A frisson of awareness tingled up her arm and she swallowed quickly. She released the other woman's hand, perversely wanting to hold it again.

This wouldn't do, she told herself. It was the height of foolishness, and Kat knew she needed to get it all into perspective. Jess Andrews was attractive but that was it. She was also straight and married. End of story, Kat told herself.

And Kat kept telling herself just that for the rest of the afternoon and evening, whenever memories of Jess Andrews's cute smile and blue eyes drifted into her mind. Then she added more air to her airbed and lay back watching her small portable TV. But Jess' attractive face seemed to drift between Kat and the screen. She'd seen far more beautiful women, so what was this fixation she had with the blond woman. She knew she didn't make a practice of preferring blonds. Until now. Both Ruth and Shael had dark hair. And they were both tall. Jess Andrews had said herself she was only five-two.

But her smile was amazing. And those bright blue eyes made Kat think of warm, summery days with sunshine on water under clear Australian skies. Kat groaned. Any moment now she'd be searching for paper and a pencil and composing poetry. And she suspected that wouldn't be difficult just thinking about gazing at Jess.

She's straight, Kat repeated as she tossed and turned, trying to sleep. She tried reading and then counting sheep, but it was hours before she drifted off, only to dream about that same smile, those very blue eyes.

Loud knocking on the front door woke Kat the next morning. Disoriented, she sat up and fumbled for her wristwatch. Seven a.m. Kat tried to clear her head. She never woke this late. It was obviously the result of a fitful sleep, troubled by those crazy, arousing dreams of Jess Andrews. The very married Jess Andrews, she kept reminding herself each time she'd shocked herself into wakefulness.

The knock came again, and Kat pushed herself to her feet. Running a hand through her tousled hair, she hurried out of the bedroom and across the living room. "Just a minute," she called, wondering if Em had decided to visit a few days early. She swung the door open only to see the smiling face that had haunted her dreams.

Kat flushed as scenes of smooth skin, a tangle of arms and legs and those soft inviting lips resurfaced from her dreams. She also realized she was standing there barefoot, wearing sagging, faded old shorts and a misshapen, equally old T-shirt. Maybe her outfit could pass for working gear. Kat hoped so and tried to be as nonchalant as she could.

"Morning," Jess said brightly, then her smile faded a little. "We didn't wake you, did we?"

"Ah, no. Not really." So the working gear scenario had failed miserably, Kat reflected. "I was just, well, relaxing and trying to plan my day." Kat stepped back. "Come on in."

"This is Lucas." Jess indicated the man who followed her into the house. "Kat Oldfield, meet my cousin and business partner, Lucas Petersen."

"Hi! Nice to meet you, Kat." Lucas shook Kat's hand. He was fair and slight like Jess, but nearly a foot taller, and their family resemblance was obvious. Kat smiled at the handsome man and her gaydar sounded. She was pretty sure Lucas Petersen was gay.

"Sorry we're so early," Lucas continued, "but I have an emergency job I need to get to as soon as I can." He looked around at Kat's unfurnished living room, the inflatable bed through the open bedroom door, and he grinned. "Ah, you're roughing it. Now that's a lot of fun."

Kat laughed. "Well, I have to say, fun in moderation. I moved out of a fully furnished flat, and I haven't had time to go out and get furniture yet."

"Renovations are easier in an unfurnished place," put in Jess.

Lucas stood, hands on slim hips, and took in the rest of the room. He nodded slowly in appreciation. "Jess said this was a beauty and she was right."

Jess pointed at the ceiling. "What do you think?"

Lucas smiled again. "Oh, yes. I think we might find some treasure under there."

Jess grinned at Kat. "Bear with us. We love our job, and we get pretty excited sometimes. Especially when there's a chance we might find some of the original house intact."

Lucas crossed into the kitchen and down the hall. He murmured and returned. "This is wonderful. Let's cross our fingers about the ceiling. I'll just get up there, if I may, and have a look. Can I borrow your ladder over there?"

"Sure." Kat shrugged.

They followed him, watched as he climbed the ladder, slid the roof access panel aside and took the flashlight from its clip on his belt. He shoved his head into the roof cavity and then hoisted himself upwards. They listened as he moved around. He sneezed and Kat grimaced.

"Don't worry," Jess assured her. "Lucas is used to this."

After a while he rejoined them and stood dusting off his shorts and shirt. Jess picked a cobweb from his hair. "So, what did you see?"

"I saw the original pressed metal ceiling. Well, actually, the back of it, but I felt it. Part of the ceiling rose is missing and I could get my hand in and feel it. Hopefully we can save it." He looked up at the ceiling. "That will have to go though."

Kat looked from Jess to her cousin and Jess laughed. "I've brought you a couple of books to have a look at." She took them from her briefcase, flipped through one to the place she'd marked and showed it to Kat. "This is what we think we'll find underneath that ceiling. Beautiful, isn't it?"

Twenty minutes later Jess and her cousin had left, Lucas reassuring Kat that the lining in the veranda wasn't the dreaded asbestos so she was free to work on it herself. Lucas did suggest wearing a protective mask and goggles anyway. There would be plenty of dust in the air once she started pulling out the cladding. He jogged down to the van and returned with a few masks and a pair of plastic protective glasses, telling her she could return the glasses to Jess when she'd finished.

After they left Kat had a quick breakfast and changed into her work clothes. No time like the present—one of Em's mother's sayings—and picked up her tools.

It was hard physical work but Kat welcomed it. Each night she fell into bed pleasantly exhausted, leaving her no time to reflect on anything. Previously her restless nights had been filled with thoughts of what she saw as the multitude of her life's failures. And in her opinion her bad track record with relationships had begun at birth.

With sixteen years difference between Kat and her only sister Beth, Kat had recognized quite early in her life that she had been a very inconvenient and unwelcome addition to her family. Her mother had seen Kat as an interruption to her career, and her father had decided Kat was the sole cause of his wife's ongoing dissatisfaction with her life, and therefore, his life. Kat's sister, Beth, had left home before Kat started school so she'd had little contact with her as she grew up.

Her upbringing had been adequate, if somewhat indifferent, and Kat had wanted to move out as soon as possible, like her elder sister. She'd really looked forward to going to university so she could do just that.

She'd been in the process of making plans to share a house with Em and a couple of other students when she met Ruth. She'd had to disappoint Em about the house as Ruth had insisted Kat move into her flat with her. In retrospect she knew she'd let Em down appallingly, but she couldn't deny she had been impressed by Ruth's wonderful unit with its expansive views and expensive furniture.

Unfortunately Ruth had also made Kat promise that she keep the fact that they were living together a secret. Ruth even forbade her to tell Em and Kat's sudden distance from Em had almost severed their long-standing friendship.

Kat and Em had been on non-speaking terms for weeks until Em had baled Kat up in the computer room and demanded Kat tell her what was going on with her. Eventually, she buckled under Em's relentless questions and had admitted she was involved with someone.

"Involved?" Em's eyes grew round and her voice dropped to a whisper. "You mean romantically?"

Kat had nodded, wishing she could tell Em how wonderful Ruth was, but Ruth had sworn her to secrecy.

"Who is it? Do I know him?" Em asked excitedly.

"No, not exactly," Kat began.

"Not exactly?" Em raised her eyebrows. "Come on, Kat. I either know him or I don't. Is he in our year?"

"Well, no."

"He's older then? What's he like? Handsome? Rich?" Em persisted.

Kat pulled herself together. "Yes. Really nice. Yes. And I don't care about money."

Em processed Kat's replies. "Kat, what's going on?"

"We're sort of keeping it a secret for a while."

"A secret?" Em's eyebrows rose again, and she clasped her hand over her mouth. "Oh, Mary Mother of God! He's married, isn't he? Kat this isn't a good idea. In fact, this is a very bad idea."

"That's not it, Em. I promise."

"Then what's the problem?" Em frowned. "Why the secrecy? I'm your very best friend, Kat, so why can't you tell me?"

Kat swallowed. Em was her best friend and until now, Kat could tell her anything and everything. But would she still want to be Kat's friend if Kat told her the truth? Could Kat take that chance? She couldn't bear to lose Em's friendship.

With her own cold home life, Kat had been drawn to Em's very different family like a moth to a flame. Kat saw Em's parents and her family as her salvation. Their home was filled with the aroma of Em's mother's baking, the noise of Em's siblings, the good-natured squabbles and the laughter. Em and her family had provided Kat with a sanctuary. She desperately didn't want to lose that. But because of Ruth, Kat now knew who she was and why she had felt so different. She had to be true to herself, didn't she?

"Come on, Kat Oldfield," Em said firmly, as only Em could. "Time to come clean, don't you think?"

Kat glanced around. They were alone in the computer room so she closed the door and motioned for Em to sit down. "You're right. There is something I need to talk to you about, Em."

"I knew it. I've known for a couple of weeks there was something going on with you."

"It's been longer than that, I think," Kat began and paused. She swallowed again, feeling as though her throat was constricting. "You know when we've been growing up how I've been, well, different to you, Em."

"Different? How? You mean you're Protestant and I'm Catholic? That's not all that different, Kat." Em waved her hand dismissively. "It was just the luck of the draw."

"No. Not that. It was more about, well," Kat swallowed painfully again, "guys, I guess."

"Guys? What about them?" Em frowned. "You've never liked guys much. I mean, you never used to get crushes like the rest of us. You were too sensible, Kat. My mother was always holding you up to me as an example." Em rolled her eyes. "If I heard 'Why can't you be sensible like Kat' from Mum once, I heard it a thousand times. Every time I drooled over a boy Mum would shake her head and remind me that you never did things like that."

"I'm sorry about that, Em, but didn't you ever wonder why I didn't?"

Em's brow furrowed. "You were just shy. You'd go all quiet and standoffish and, of course, all the guys would be so intrigued they'd try harder to get your attention. If you ask me it was a brilliant ploy, and you could have used it so much more than you did."

"It wasn't a conscious thing, Em. I just didn't, well, quite honestly they didn't do anything for me."

Em laughed. "Well, now that we have so many more for comparison, the guys in our circle back then weren't all that hot, so I can see where you're coming from there."

"That's not quite what I mean." Kat took a deep breath. "I think, I mean I know, I prefer women," she finished quickly.

"You prefer women," Em repeated.

For long seconds Em was silent, and Kat imagined she could see her friend's mind change gear, saw the moment the truth became clear. Kat's muscles seemed to tighten. She barely breathed.

A dull flush colored Em's face. "Women. Women?" she repeated and gasped in disbelief. "You're a lesbian? Kat, you have to be mistaken. You can't, well, you don't look like a lesbian. I mean, you're not masculine and your hair's not all that short, and, well, I'm your best friend and I would have known."

Kat remained silent.

"Kat, you can't be. Just because you don't like guys doesn't mean you're a lesbian. What makes you think you are?" Em stopped and gasped. "You mean the person you're involved with is a woman?" she asked incredulously.

Kat nodded. "Yes. It's a woman."

"Who is it?"

"I don't want to say, Em. She's, well, not exactly out."

"Out? Oh, out. As a lesbian, you mean?"

Kat nodded again. "Em, I'm sorry I didn't tell you before because I, well, I didn't know how you'd feel about it. As you said, you are my best friend, and I didn't, I don't want to lose you." Kat swallowed as a knot of tears stuck in her throat.

"Lose me? What are you on about, Kat Oldfield?" Em leaned over and gave Kat a hug. "As a friend I'm made of sterner stuff than that. Remember how we always vowed when we were kids that we'd be friends through thick and thin, and we'd never let anything come between us."

Tears did trickle down Kat's cheek and Em made clucking sounds, hugging Kat again. "Oh, Em, I was terrified I'd lose you over this."

"Well, you haven't. Although if you don't tell me who it is I might reconsider," she threatened, and Kat gave a half laugh.

"I really love you, Em." Kat laughed again. "I mean like a sister. Actually, I love you more than my sister."

"So what you're saying is you're not attracted to me then?"

"Not in that way," Kat reassured her.

"Hmmm. I don't know whether to be wounded or relieved."

They laughed together, then Em looked seriously at Kat.

"Have you, you know, slept with her?"

It was Kat's turn to blush. "I can't talk to you about this, Em. Well, not yet anyway."

"I'll take that as a yes." Em's expression was thoughtful. "So what do lesbians do? I mean, guys have, you know. And women don't. If you know what I mean."

"A good Catholic girl isn't supposed to know about all that."

"This one does. Well, in theory," Em added dryly. She frowned again. "And talking about that, the Bible doesn't exactly heap blessings on homosexuals, Kat. What about that?"

Kat thought about her feelings for Ruth. "I can't see a god being so against love, Em. Hate's the far more worrying emotion."

"Hmm. I should ask Father David."

"And what if Father David is so concerned about your

questions he thinks you're referring to yourself, and he talks to your parents about it?" Kat said and watched a range of different emotions play over her friend's expressive face.

"Do you think?" she asked at last and pulled a face. "Hmmm. Then again, maybe not." Em held her hands up in capitulation. "Perhaps it's best we don't know for sure. Let's let sleeping dogs lie in that case, because if Mum and Dad question me I might let slip about you. You know how good they are at weaseling things out of me."

"Like the time you talked me into going to that party when we were supposed to be at each other's houses studying?" Kat reminded her friend.

"I wish you'd give over about that, Kat. But yes, just like that."

"Look, Em. I don't mind if you tell your mother. I don't want to make you uncomfortable keeping things from her."

"But what if you decide you aren't a lesbian? That would make it far too complicated."

"I'm not going to do that, Em. I am a lesbian," Kat said levelly.

"Are you going to tell your own parents?"

Kat shrugged. "I want to. But I don't think they'll be as liberal as you are about it."

"Perhaps not. Maybe you could tell Beth, and she could tell your parents. I always found that worked pretty well for me. I'd just tell Bernadine and make myself scarce for a while, give Mum and Dad time to cool down."

Kat laughed. "You are absolutely incorrigible, Margaret Mary Martin."

Em grinned broadly. "I know. But I'd really like to meet her, Kat. Your girlfriend, I mean."

"I'd like you to meet her, too. I'll ask her and see what she thinks."

At least when Em and Ruth met the meeting had been far more civil than the one with Kat's parents.

A few weeks after the horrible incident with her parents Kat had tentatively asked Ruth if she could ask Em over to the unit. Surprisingly Ruth had agreed, if somewhat reluctantly. Although initially Ruth had remarked dryly that if Em was anything like Kat's family they might be in for a jolly old time justifying alternative lifestyles. Kat had assured Ruth that Em wasn't at all like that. Ruth had laughed and kissed her and told Kat she had no intention of keeping her from her friends.

Initially, the meeting had been strained, with Em calling Ruth "Professor Dunleavy," and giving every appearance of being a nervous student. Kat had sent an appealing gaze across the table at Ruth, who rolled her eyes and set about encouraging Em to relax. Ruth asked questions, and Em started talking and that was that. Although Em and Ruth had never been friends, Em had thawed a little towards the other woman.

Em's attitude had been along the lines of, "I don't know what you see in her when you could have any number of guys who were waiting to be encouraged, but whatever."

Of course, Em's mother had somehow managed to loosen Em's tongue and Em had apologetically warned Kat about it as they drove in Em's old car on their next visit to the Martins. "You know how Mum is, Kat," Em said remorsefully. "She'd get a confession out of the most hardened of criminals."

"And that doesn't run in the family much, hmmm? But is your mother likely to mention it?" Kat had asked, a sinking feeling in her stomach. Somehow the thought of having the Martins banish her from their home caused far more emotional turmoil in Kat than being ostracized by her own family. "How did she sound? Was she horrified? I mean, how did she react?"

"Kat, stop! You're making my head spin. And that's not ideal when I'm driving," Em said. "Stop worrying, Kat. She wasn't horrified. But she was surprised. Good grief! Who wouldn't be? Even I was surprised."

"I don't know why you were." Kat sighed. "I've always been different."

"Everyone knew different, Kat. But not lesbian." Em turned into the Martin driveway. "And certainly not having an affair with an older professor who happens to be a woman. Can I just say, Kat? If, as you're always saying, you've lived a boring, conforming life so far, then you're sure making up for it now in the nonconforming stakes."

"I didn't mean to, Em. It just happened. And I'm not having an affair with Ruth. I'm in love with her."

They sat in the car and Em looked across at Kat. "I know you are, love," she said gently. "But I'm just worried that she doesn't feel the same way about you. There have been rumors and I don't want you to get hurt. That's all."

"I know, Em. But it's all good. Ruth admits she's played the field, but we love each other." And at that time Kat genuinely believed it was true.

Kat had been on tenterhooks for the first part of Sunday dinner with the Martins but when no one made any comments she relaxed and enjoyed the atmosphere as she always did. As she laughed at a joke one of Em's brother's told them she had a sudden picture of Ruth, sitting at the huge table in the midst of this boisterous family, and she knew Ruth would hate every moment of it. There was no way Ruth could share this part, this huge part, of Kat's life. It was a sobering thought she pushed to the back of her mind.

Later when Kat was helping Mrs. Martin with the dishes, Em's mother sent her two youngest out to their father and turned to Kat. "Now we're alone, love," she said, dropping her voice, "there's something I feel I should talk to you about."

Knowing what was coming Kat tensed, her eyes desperately trying to gauge Em's mother's expression.

"Em told me. About Ruth Dunleavy."

"I—Em shouldn't have mentioned it," Kat began.

"You know Em, love. She's too open. Especially when she's got a worry on her mind. So don't blame her, she's simply concerned about you."

"There's no need for Em to worry. Or you. I'm fine. I can't, well, I can't change what I am." Kat twisted the tea towel in her fingers.

"I know you can't." Em's mother sighed. "And nobody should ask you to."

"You don't mind? Me being a lesbian, I mean. You don't want me to stop coming here?"

"Of course not, love. Why would I want that? We all love you."

And then Kat was in Em's mother's arms, sobbing into her shoulder, holding on to her as though she were a ship needing an anchor in a storm. Em's mother rubbed Kat's back, murmured soothingly the way she'd done for Kat and all the Martin children since Kat had known her.

Eventually Kat stood back, took the tissue Em's mother passed her. "I'm sorry. I just thought you mightn't want me here and that you might not want me to stay friends with Em."

"Never in a million years, Kat." Em's mother patted Kat's cheek. "And I'm sure Em would have something to say about that. Sit down, love."

They sat opposite each other in the breakfast nook. "I can't say I understand what being a lesbian is like, Kat, but it can't be an easy life. There are still a lot of people who feel strongly opposed to it. They're not always rational people, so I guess I'm concerned for your safety."

"I don't tell everyone. If they ask I do, but what I'm trying to say is I'm not a very visible lesbian. It's, well, fairly new to me, knowing that I am a lesbian, so I'm still getting used to it all. But it is right for me," Kat said earnestly.

Em's mother nodded. "And you do have a relationship with Ruth Dunleavy?"

Kat nodded. "It was— I can't explain it. She's wonderful. Funny. Intelligent. Attractive. I love her so much."

Em's mother paused, obviously choosing her words carefully. "If you're going around with Ruth then I'm afraid you will be visible, Kat. Ruth's a known lesbian. She always has been."

"Well." Kat swallowed. "I can't change what's in the past. I just know we love each other now."

"Then I hope it all works out for you both. I just want you to know I'm here, we're all here, if you need anything, Kat, day or night. You're part of the family, you know."

"Thank you. That means a lot to me. Did Em tell you my parents refused to see me again until I come to my senses?" Kat gave a rueful laugh. "Like that's going to happen."

"Give them time to get it all into perspective. It's hard on parents. We still see you as children, and it takes a little longer for some people to recognize that their children are now all grown up and making their own decisions and way in life."

"I wish I was a Martin," Kat said and then laughed a little self consciously. "When we were young I was always asking Em to ask you if you'd adopt me."

"What? You'd choose to be part of this rambunctious lot?"

"Yes," Kat said honestly. "Always."

Em's mother squeezed Kat's hand and quickly wiped a tear from her eye. "You are part of the family, Kat. You call me anytime if you need to talk."

And when Kat had told Ruth about her conversation with Em's mother and she came to the part where everyone in the area had known Ruth was a lesbian, Ruth had raised her fine dark eyebrows. "The so-notorious Ruth Dunleavy, hmm? Next thing we know there'll be roadblocks to keep me from entering the precinct. Maybe you don't want to be seen with me any more?"

Kat had gone to her, pulled her into a fierce embrace. "No way. I'll just have to be notorious, too."

Ruth stepped back a little. "Fortunately, there's no need for us to go anywhere near the old hometown now." She frowned. "And perhaps we should put any more coming out to all and sundry on hold for a while, keep our relationship a little more low-key."

Kat felt a jolt of fear. What did Ruth mean? Did she want Kat to move out? Everyone said Ruth rarely stayed in a relationship for long, that she moved on as easily as she began a relationship. Even Ruth's friends had teased Kat about that. One had even likened Ruth to the honeybee in the *King and I*. Flitting from flower to flower, the honeybee had to be free. Kat swallowed.

"I mean, let's stay in more," Ruth continued. "I'm sure we could find something to do to entertain ourselves, don't you?"

Ruth and Kat had been together for nearly six years before Ruth had strayed. And they'd never returned to the suburb where they were brought up. Well, Ruth hadn't. But Kat still visited the Martins whenever she could.

Now here Kat was, back in the district, in Ruth's house, the house that was now hers. Her parents lived only streets away, but Kat had no intention of opening any dialogue with them.

So, for the rest of the week Kat worked herself to a standstill and slept dreamlessly. It was when she stopped for a coffee break or a quick meal that her thoughts seemed to turn to the cute Jess

Andrews. It was perfectly harmless, she justified, and far more positive than thinking about Shael. There were no expectations regarding Jess. Kat knew there was no future with her. She was straight and apparently happily married. She probably even had a bundle of kids. And although Kat was sure Grace Worrall would fill her in, each time Grace appeared with afternoon tea and homemade cookies Kat managed to restrain herself from asking questions about Jess.

Kat believed that thinking about Jess was far healthier than chastising herself about bad choices and failed relationships. There was no chance they'd even get to a relationship so there wouldn't be the chance to fail. Her life would remain on a completely straight and unbending highway with no choices and none of Em's so-called forks in the road. And no pun intended regarding the straight road, Kat said out loud to amuse herself. She told herself all was well, but— That small pang of genuine regret lingered on two fronts, regret for what could have been if Jess was a lesbian and regret that Kat had such a bad track record when it came to relationships.

She stood up and flexed her stiff back. Time to end her coffee break. She reached for her work gloves and turned as a car pulled into the driveway. Kat grinned as Em climbed from her purple VW bug. Her dark curls shone in the sunlight as she looked from the house to Kat.

"Good grief! I could almost wish I was a lesbian you look so deliciously butch in that getup," she said as she walked up the steps.

"And hello to you too," Kat said dryly. "You're early. I wasn't expecting you till lunch so I thought I had plenty of time to get cleaned up."

"I'm really glad you didn't. You look fantastic, love. Fit. Healthy. Alive." Em regarded her. "In fact, you look like a different person."

"I'm afraid I'm not. I'm still the same old same old." Kat gave her friend a peck on the cheek. "I'll give you a welcoming hug after I've had a shower. I'd hate to mess up that glorious outfit you're almost wearing."

Em giggled. "Bit revealing, isn't it? I'm sure the top wasn't as low cut when I tried it on before I bought it. Joe likes it though."

"I'll just bet he does. You look wonderful."

"Good enough to eat, hmm?" Em waggled her eyebrows and Kat groaned.

"You know, sometimes I really regret coming out to you."

"No you don't. And I already knew you were anyway." Em followed Kat up the steps. "I knew when we were at high school."

"You did not know in high school. I wasn't even sure myself then. As I recall I told you at Uni and you were so surprised you were speechless. One of the few times that happened, that's for sure," Kat added in amusement.

"Very funny, oh Kat of the long, long memory. If I'd known the symptoms of lesbianism when we were in high school I'd have seen you as a prime candidate."

"Symptoms?" Kat shook her head in disbelief. "It's not a disease, Em."

Em laughed easily. "I know. I was just teasing. And it did cross my mind once before you told me. It was when that Luke Margolis started trying to get your attention. Remember him? All dark and brooding. The rest of us were so jealous and you just acted as though you didn't even notice."

"Yes, I remember him and it wasn't an act, Em. I really didn't notice."

"I know, but that's when Sue asked me if you were gay. I told her in no uncertain terms that you weren't and gave her a major lecture on starting rumors."

"Sue thought I was gay?" Kat gave a half laugh. "Then I wish you'd told me what she'd said. Maybe it would have saved me a lot of angst."

"A bit of angst is good for the soul, so they say."

"The ubiquitous they who have never suffered any angst at all, you mean?"

"Probably." Em laughed. "Wow! The house is wonderful. I think." She looked around her. "Aren't you going to renovate it? It looks like you're pulling it down?"

"Only some of it. I'm opening it up so the veranda's back to the original one."

"Oh. Kat, I'm impressed. Give me the grand tour."

After they'd looked around Kat hurried into the shower, leaving Em to make a cup of tea. After her shower she pulled on a pair of denim shorts and a snug sleeveless tank top and rejoined Em as she finished toweling her hair dry.

"Happiness is clean, dust-free hair." Kat said. "Oh, and the rest of me, too," she added, peering out from under the towel. She paused as she realized Em wasn't alone. A familiar khaki-clad figure sat in one of the four comfy chairs Kat had bought from a secondhand shop. "Jess! Hello! I didn't hear you arrive," she said and suspected she was blushing. One glance at Em's raised eyebrows confirmed her suspicions.

Jess smiled her incredible smile and indicated the manila envelope on Kat's new coffee table. "I have your quotes so I thought I'd drop them off on my way back to the office." She took a sip of tea Em had made her.

"Thanks. That was quick."

"We aim to please. I'll leave it with you to look over then we can get together to discuss it if you want to go ahead with the work."

"Great. I—" Kat glanced at Em again. "I guess you two have introduced yourselves."

"We have." Em grinned. "I told Jess I was your best friend and that I know all your secrets."

Kat draped the wet towel over the windowsill and ran her fingers through her damp hair. "Let's call the newspapers. My secrets should keep the public enthralled for, oh, about sixty seconds."

Jess laughed and the sound rippled through Kat and warmed her heart.

"I know you're far more interesting than that, Kat," Jess said, and Kat saw Em's expressive eyebrows rise again.

"Ain't that the truth," Em agreed cryptically. "So you renovate old houses too?" She focused on Jess.

"Not quite. I'm the person who talks money," she replied easily. "But I also love seeing a property like this transformed. Just the way Kat's opened up the veranda has made such a difference already."

Em looked around skeptically. "I guess. I'm afraid I like bricks and mortar, quite literally."

Jess shrugged. "I like houses like that, too. I suppose it's not the appearance so much as the people living inside the house."

"Yes. That's right. Families in all their very diverse forms."

"Is that my tea, Em?" Kat asked, feeling the need to sidetrack her. Kat loved her dearly, but she never knew what Em would say next.

Em added a spoonful of sugar to Kat's tea and passed the mug to her. "Here you are, love. Just the way you like it." She gave Kat a covert smile.

Kat sent her friend a warning look. Not that it should matter what Jess thought of her or how she perceived the situation. It wasn't as though she was trying to make an impression. Kat gave herself a mental shake before sitting down and sipping her tea.

"Much more comfortable." Jess said, indicating the new old easy chairs.

Kat nodded. "Now I just have to address the bed situation. I think I'm getting too old to sleep on the floor."

"I should say so," put in Em, crossing one of her shapely legs over the other.

And Kat was sure Jess noticed.

"What if you wanted to entertain," Em continued blithely.

"Entertain?" Kat's mind turned slowly and she frowned.

"Yes. Entertain." Em made the sign for quotation marks with one hand. "As in, bring someone home for dinner and, well, whatever."

Kat flushed again. "Oh, I'm far too busy at the moment to do any entertaining. Apart from that," she rushed on, "I'm not much of a cook."

Em opened her mouth, only to pause when Jess spoke.

"I'm the same. I can usually turn out something adequate, but my friends don't exactly flock around when they know I'm cooking. Lucas is the cook in the family."

"Ah. It's nice to have a husband who can cook. My Joe would live on frozen meals if I wasn't there."

"Oh, Lucas isn't my husband. He's my cousin. He owns part of our family business."

"And is this Lucas good-looking and, more importantly, single?" asked Em.

Kat slid a glance at Jess. She was sure she saw a flash of indecision cross Jess's face. Kat knew she'd suspected Lucas was gay. Could it be that was a problem for Jess?

"He is really good looking," Jess replied casually. "But, no, Lucas *is* in a relationship. Pity, isn't it?" she added with a quick smile.

"Darn!" Em exclaimed. "He would have suited Kat to a tee."

Jess's blue eyes met Kat's and Kat swallowed. What would Jess be thinking now? She'd have to have a serious word with Em. She was giving out so many mixed messages it would be making Jess's head spin.

"Can I get you another cup of tea, Jess?" Kat stood up.

Jess shook her head, standing up too. "No, thanks." She set her empty mug on the breakfast bar. "I have to keep moving. I've got a couple more jobs to check on before I go back to the office." She started for the door.

"I'll look over the quotes tonight and ring you in the morning," Kat said and Jess nodded.

"Sure. I'll look forward to hearing from you. Nice meeting you, Em. And thanks again for the tea. 'Bye for now."

"Well!" Em said when they heard the front gate close. "She is *very* cute."

"Em! For heaven's sake! Give me a break!" Kat sat down again. "Unless she desperately wants my business, I'd say she'd have the pedal to the metal making a quick getaway."

"Why would she want to do that?" Em asked innocently.

"Well, for starters, at the beginning of that crazy conversation she'd have to be forgiven for thinking you were a lesbian and we were a couple."

"A lesbian couple? Why would she think that? I mentioned I had a husband, Joe."

"Eventually! Which would have been the only thing that stopped her from running screaming. I've never seen so much eyelid-batting and leg-crossing and the sun isn't even over the yardarm."

"I thought the yardarm was to do with imbibing? But all that aside, do you think she was interested?" Em asked with a grin.

"Em, listen to yourself. You're the kind of straight woman who gives straight women a bad name. And just as Jess was relaxing, you shift into overdrive and put it out that I'm in the market, the heterosexual market, for a new man. What was all that about me being a huge man-eating threat to her poor unfortunate cousin Lucas? Who, I might add, is exceptionally good-looking and is almost certainly as gay as all get out."

"Must run in the family." Em put her finger to her cheek and frowned. "It has to be genetic, you know."

Kat's eyebrows rose in surprise. "What are you talking about, Em?"

"Well, that there must be a gene or a chromosome or something because so often you get more than one member of a family who's gay and—"

"No, not the gene thing—"

"And Lucas and Jess are cousins," Em continued imperviously, "and they're both gay. Do you think Beth's gay?"

"My sister's married," Kat put in.

"But she was single until she was nearly forty, and she had lots of female friends."

"She worked in an all-female office and was building her career." Kat sighed loudly. "But we're not talking about Beth."

"I know but—"

"You know, following your conversations can be as exhausting as spending a session at the gym."

"Well, I wouldn't know about that," Em said dismissively. "I can't cope with gyms and all they entail. All that perspiration and testosterone and unflattering lycra." Em paused. "But on the other hand—"

"Em!"

Em chuckled. "Okay. Now, where were we? Oh, yes. Back to the very attractive Jess. I was saying she was as gay as you were saying her cousin is."

"Sorry to disappoint you, Miss Know-it-all, but Jess Andrews is married."

Em pursed her lips skeptically. "She is? Did she tell you that?"

"Well, no. But she didn't have to. I can't believe your eagle eyes missed seeing the ring, the gold band, on her telling finger." Kat held up her left hand and wiggled her ring finger. "And," she went on when Em would have commented, "her husband's the nephew of the Worralls next door. They, well, Grace Worrall actually, recommended the company when I said I needed some help with the renovations. Jess and her husband and her cousin Lucas own the business."

"Married. Hmm?" Em gave it a moment's thought. "Well, if she is straight then she's giving off some mixed messages of her own."

"I know I'm going to regret this, but what mixed messages would they be, oh message-mixing guru? And please don't say it's because she wears boots. Wearing boots does not make her a lesbian."

"No." Em sounded unconvinced. "But a lot of lesbians do wear boots. But that wasn't it. She watches you, Kat. When you're not looking." Em sat back. "I rest my case."

"She watches me?" Kat repeated incredulously fighting down the spark of pleasure that rose inside her at the thought that Em might be right. "If that's all the evidence you have, then they'd laugh your case out of court." *Unfortunately*, said the small voice inside Kat.

"It's not just that she watches you, Kat. It's the way she watches you. Know what I mean?"

Kat shifted in her seat as her body reacted to the split second of wishful thinking as she allowed herself to believe that Jess Andrews might be interested, even attracted to her. "No, I don't know what you mean," she said, as much to quell her own ridiculousness as discourage Em.

Em sighed exasperatedly. "Honestly, Kat! I don't know that it's safe to let you out alone. Just take it from me, Jess is interested in you, and it has nothing to do with the price of bricks and mortar." She waved her hand to encompass the house. "Or in this case timber and, well, whatever."

"Now isn't that going to please her husband immensely," Kat stated sarcastically.

"Mmm." Em steepled her fingers and tapped them on her

chin. "Something of a tangled web, I'll agree." She shook her head. "Not a situation you should step into lightly, Kat."

"Fortunately I have no intention of stepping into anything," Kat remarked, not acknowledging the tiny surge of regret that rose inside her again. "Lightly or not," she added for good measure.

"Probably for the best. Complications abound there. But what an absolute bummer, love, not to mention rotten luck, because even I can see how great you two could be together."

Amen to that, Kate reflected to herself and firmly changed the subject. After their conversation about Jess, she and Em had visited Em's parents and taken them out to lunch. They'd had a wonderful afternoon as Kat always did with Em's family. When they'd dropped Em's parents home, and Em had left as well, Kat had sat listening to the silence of the house. She should be doing some more work in the hour or so left before nightfall, but for the first time she'd felt a spurt of loneliness. Perhaps that's why hermits became hermits she reflected. They kept away from people because interacting with people only reminded them how lonely they were when they were alone. Oh please, *get a grip*! Preferably on the jimmy bar and get to work.

In the darkness of her room later that night, Kat sighed as she sought a comfortable spot on the airbed. In all seriousness, Kat acknowledged that although she liked some solitude, she probably would not enjoy living alone permanently. *Was that simply needy?* But she thrust that thought aside. It didn't mean she needed a lover but—

Jess Andrews's attractive face appeared in her mind and she sighed, wishing her thoughts had remained nonspecific. Here in the dark of night, the pale moonlight dancing patterns across the floor, listening to the soft creaks of the old house, it was far too easy to allow herself to contemplate Jess being here, her smooth compact body warm beside Kat. She'd turn to Kat, fingertips playing lightly over Kat's bare skin, and her soft generous mouth…sleep was a long time coming.

Kat picked up the phone next morning and turned it over in her hand. Calling Jess Andrews about her quote should be a simple business call, but Kat's tummy fluttered and she strode across the kitchen and poured herself a glass of water. She set the glass down and swore under her breath. She knew she was acting like a lovesick teenager and over a woman she'd only just met. No matter what the imaginative Em thought, Jess Andrews was way out of bounds, even if she did want to dabble on the dark side. Kat wasn't into straight women's experiments. End of story.

Taking a steadying breath, Kat punched the phone number into her mobile. When she heard Jess's voice she almost hung up.

"Ah, it's Kat. Kat Oldfield."

"Hi, Kat. How are you?"

"Fine. I've had a look at the quotes and they look fine. I do have a couple of questions though."

"Okay. Shall I call by later?"

"Well, I have a few errands to run, and I'll pass by your office. On William Street, isn't it?"

"Yes. Number Sixteen."

"I could call in to save you a trip."

"That would be great. I'm in the middle of catching up on some paperwork so I'd appreciate it. As long as you're not making a special trip."

Kat could see the smile she heard in Jess's voice, and she experienced another wave of regret. "Paperwork. That sounds exciting."

Jess did laugh then and Kat smiled too. "Very. But unfortunately necessary."

"I guess. Well, I'll probably be there in about an hour. Would that be okay?"

"Sure. I'll have the coffeepot on."

When Kat pulled her car into the carpark beneath Number 16 William Street she felt as nervous as a kitten. Ridiculous! She exclaimed out loud, feeling extremely foolish. She grabbed Jess's quote, locked the car and strode towards the elevator.

The Handy Andrews office was light, roomy and functional. At a large desk behind a computer screen sat Jess Andrews. She looked up as the door opened, and her smile widened when she saw Kat.

"Hi, Kat! Come on in." She stood up and pulled a chair up for Kat.

Kat smiled and sat down. Today Jess wore a pair of blue jeans and a short-sleeved pale blue and white checked shirt. She sat back behind the desk and ran her hand through her hair. And in that moment Kat's high-road convictions about not experimenting with the straight Jess Andrews did a fairly serious swerve and seemed in danger of crashing through the guardrail and ending up way down on the low road.

"End-of-quarter toting up," Jess said waving her hand at the computer. "What a headache."

Kat swallowed and nodded sympathetically. "I have friends who own an art gallery, and they say they have a complete character change when they do their tax statements."

"Exactly." Jess looked longingly out the window. "And for me it always seems twice as bad when it's a beautifully sunny day like today." She stood up again. "But I promised coffee. Or would you prefer tea?"

"Coffee would be fine."

"Okay. Just sit tight for a minute." Jess went over to the doorway behind her and disappeared inside.

Kat watched admiringly, wondering why certain people caught your eye while others didn't. Shael believed you always followed your predisposed body types. Kat liked tall and dark, or as Shael put it, dark and dangerous. And both Ruth and Shael had been tall and dark. As to the dangerous, well, in the end they'd both proved to be damaging to Kat's self-esteem. But, she acknowledged, they'd been similar in a lot of ways.

Yet, Jess Andrews was as different as chalk from cheese. Apart from the physical aspects, Jess was bright and bubbly and seemed to have an infectious joy of life. But hadn't she thought Ruth and Shael were bright and pleasant, too—in the beginning. And how well did she know Jess Andrews anyway? Jess was a businesswoman. Being less than pleasant to her customers would definitely be bad for business. If Kat got to know her it might well be a different story, one she told herself she'd already read and had no intention of reading again. She pulled her wayward thoughts together. Strictly business, she told herself and made herself smile as Jess returned with two mugs of coffee.

"Jeanne, our office assistant, is away for a week, and she makes far better coffee than I do."

"I'm sure it will be fine," Kat said, took a sip and nodded. "It's great."

Jess grinned. "So," she indicated the envelope Kat had rested on the desk, "what questions have you got for me?"

They discussed the quotes, and agreed on the price and Jess promised to have the contracts drawn up by the next day.

"Will you be home tomorrow afternoon? About four?" Jess asked.

"Yes. But I can call back here if it's easier for you."

"It's okay. I have to be over your way about then anyway. Oh." She reached over to the other side of her computer. "I meant to show you this." She opened a manila folder. "This is a job we've just finished. It's much like yours, and I thought it might give you an idea of our quality of workmanship."

"Perhaps I should have checked that out before I agreed to sign the contract," Kat said with a laugh. "But in my defense I did check out your references."

"Good. We do take pride in our work, I can assure you." She walked around to Kat's side of the desk and showed her some before and after photos.

Kat could almost feel the warmth of Jess's body, but she made herself concentrate on the photos and Kat was impressed. The renovation was amazing. The last photo was of the finished house. Kat murmured appreciatively.

"The final painting makes so much difference, doesn't it?"

"That's outstanding. Seeing this makes me want to get started immediately." She returned the folder of photographs to Jess. "We didn't talk about a time frame, did we?"

"We have a few teams of subcontractors working with us, and we have a week of smaller jobs to do but one big one we were due to make a start on has had to be postponed for a month. The owner broke his leg rather badly falling off his son's dirt bike, and his wife has decided he needs time to recuperate before we remodel their house. So we can start Monday week as long as the plans come back from city council. We'll submit them ASAP. How's that?"

"Great. And if you can list the things I need to finish demolishing to be ready for your start, that would be good."

"Well, seeing as you're living at the house I suggest we do the en suite in the back bedroom before we demolish the other bathroom. That will be the least intrusive for you." Jess put the manila folder back down on her desk as she crossed to take her seat.

The folder knocked over a framed photograph that was standing on the desk, and Kat picked it up to right it. She glanced at it as she stood it back up on the desk. It showed two smiling children in a studio portrait.

Jess was smiling again. "My kids."

"Oh." Kat studied the photo.

"Look like angels there." Jess laughed. "But they do have their moments."

"How old are they?" Kat asked.

"Miranda's ten and Caleb's eight. That photo was taken a couple of months ago."

The girl was dark and the boy fair like Jess. Kat glanced back at Jess. She scarcely looked old enough to have an eight-year-old, let alone a ten-year-old and Kat said as much.

"Well, many thanks. I'm thirty-five." Jess laughed.

Kat was surprised. "I would have said early to mid-twenties."

"Oh, many, many thanks then. Don't they say kids keep you young?" Jess shook her head. "Funny though, sometimes they make me feel fifty."

Kat laughed. "Well, they're very cute and attractive kids." *Just like their mother*, Kat wanted to add.

"Must take after their father," said a deep voice behind Kat and she turned around.

A dark-haired man had entered the office and strode towards them. He wore similar light khaki shorts and shirt to the outfit Jess had worn when she first came out to the house. He was smiling, and Kat had to admit he was very attractive. He had the classic, chiseled features of the type of model who advertised outdoorsy products and adventures, soft drinks or four-wheel drives heading out over rough terrain. He looked fit and vital.

No wonder the Andrews children were so attractive. They came from an extremely attractive gene pool.

"They get their beauty from me and their brains from their mother," he said with a self-derisive laugh. He held out his hand and Kat automatically shook it. "I'm Mark Andrews and you must be Kat Oldfield. Jess has told me all about you."

"She has?" Kat slid a glance at Jess but couldn't quite decipher the fleeting expression on Jess's face.

"Talked about nothing else," said Mark Andrews easily. "She's been itching to work on that house of yours for years. We can see her eying it every time we visit Tom and Grace next door."

"I might have mentioned once or twice that it had potential," Jess said dryly. "Anyway, Kat's given us the go-ahead to start on the renovations."

"Fantastic." Mark smiled. "I was going to say that we're the best in the business, but no doubt Jess has told you that already, too."

"She did say something like that." Kat smiled at Jess and she shrugged.

"Good. And it's all true." He turned to Jess. "I just called in for that invoice for Bob Jefferson."

Jess lifted a pile of papers, sorted through them and handed it to her husband.

"Thanks, love. Well, Kat, nice to meet you. No doubt we'll run into each other on the job site."

"Yes. Nice to meet you too." Kat said with a sinking heart. That was a propitious meeting, she told herself. A handsome husband was more than enough incentive to keep it strictly business between herself and Jess Andrews.

"See you later," he said and Kat watched as Jess's husband gave a smile and left them.

Kat replaced the photo of the Andrews children on the desk. "Well." She made herself smile. "I see now why the children are so attractive. You and your husband are very good-looking."

"Thank you." Jess gave a crooked smile. "And actually, Mark's my ex-husband."

CHAPTER FOUR

"Oh. I'm—I'm sorry. I thought—"

Jess grimaced. "No need to be sorry. We aren't. Mark and I are far better friends and business associates than we ever were as husband and wife."

"How long were you married?"

"Hmm. The jury's out there." Jess laughed, although Kat couldn't be sure there was no underlying bitterness. "We've been officially divorced for six years or so."

Ex plus husband. So what difference did the ex make, Kat asked herself as she drove home. Ex or not, that still meant Jess had been married. On top of that, Mark Andrews was obviously still in the picture. And although Jess hadn't said why they'd divorced, Kat couldn't quite see that the fact Jess was a lesbian would be the reason for their breakup. Mark Andrews didn't look like a man whose marriage had broken down because his wife changed her sexual orientation. But, then again, she told herself, who would know looking in from the outside. Still, for a lesbian intent upon an uncomplicated life, a husband, even in the ex category, made Jess off limits as far as Kat was concerned.

However, Jess Andrews didn't look like a lesbian, no matter what Em had said. And what did a lesbian look like? Kat asked herself with a grudging laugh. She'd been told she didn't look like a lesbian either. In fact, Shael's mother had confided in Kat that she was so pleased Kat was sharing a house with her daughter and granddaughter because Kat didn't look like a lesbian so people wouldn't talk. If only there was a secret handshake or an "L" on foreheads that only other lesbians could see. It would sure take the guesswork out of the equation. X + Y + L on a forehead = Lesbian.

Kat giggled and then stopped, suspecting she was bordering on the hysterical. At this rate if she didn't keep her mind on her driving, she'd crash her car. And she could see the headlines now. *DISTURBING INCIDENT ON CITY STREET. A car crashed into a light pole on a city street today. No one was injured in the mysterious accident, but an unidentified woman was seen running from the scene. A witness told police the woman was extremely attractive*—Kat giggled again—*and seemed to have an unusual L-shaped marking on her forehead.*

Kat's chuckle turned into a full-fledged laugh. *And we'd have to say the witness was obviously suffering from a serious case of denial.* Kat stopped for a red light, still laughing, then sobered when she noticed the driver in the car beside hers eyed her strangely. She drove on, telling herself the best medicine for a case of hysteria was to go straight home and knock down another wall. And please, she implored herself, no comments about going *straight* home. She laughed again, realizing she hadn't laughed so heartily at herself for a long time. She was still smiling when she parked the car under the house.

She changed into her work gear and stood trying to decide

which section on the veranda she should attack next, but only half her attention was on the job. She kept playing over the time she'd spent at Jess's office and her meeting with Jess's ex-husband. When her phone suddenly rang she answered quickly, thinking it might be Jess.

"Kat, it's Shael," said a familiar voice.

"Oh!" Kat's body stiffened. What would Shael want? From previous experience it wasn't usually anything Kat wanted. "Hello," she said reluctantly. She heard an irritated sigh.

"It's about Megghan."

"Meggie? What's wrong with her?" Kat asked, concerned now.

"Nothing's wrong with her. You're such a pessimist, Kat. Megghan," Shael emphasized the name, "is fine. Well, fine, apart from driving me insane about coming to stay with you. And that's what I wanted to discuss with you, to see if you're free this weekend?"

"Of course." Kat tried not to sound too excited. "I told you she could come anytime."

Shael paused. "Megghan says you're not at the flat anymore, that you're living in the house Ruth left you."

"That's right," Kat said carefully.

"She also tells me, with great excitement I might add, that you have no furniture."

"I do now. And I'm fixing the house up."

"Well, from memory the house needs a considerable amount of fixing up. And it's way out of town."

"Not that far. From the CBD it's about ten minutes further than where we lived."

"I meant it's across town," Shael said shortly. "And that presents a problem. Can you come over and collect Megghan? I don't think I'll have time to drive way out there."

Kat thought about Jess and the appointment they had about the contract. "Well, I can if it's a little later. I have an appointment with the builders at four."

"So what time do you think you'll be here?"

"Probably seven. Maybe a little earlier."

"I'd appreciate it, Kat, if you can get here earlier. Tori and I have to leave by seven forty-five at the latest to make our flight."

"I see."

"We're going to Sydney for a break. Tori— We've both been tired and need to get away. We'll be back late on Monday so will it be all right if Megghan stays until Tuesday?"

"Of course. If she wants to," Kat added.

Shael gave a short laugh. "Oh, it's fine with Megghan," she said a little bitterly. "So. I'll see you tomorrow night."

"Yes. And Shael. Thanks."

"Kat, don't—" Shael sighed again. "Okay. Goodbye then."

Kat raced out to a local furniture shop and bought a new bed ensemble with the stipulation that it be delivered the next day. She also bought a stand to replace the wooden packing case that held her television and by the time she had it all set up next day Kat felt that, even with the part-demolition of the veranda, the place was beginning to feel like home. And more importantly, it was a place where she could share her time with Meggie.

Kat finished up early and had a shower. She pulled on her best jeans and a light green fitted T-shirt with three-quarter sleeves.

As she brushed her hair she paused, looked at her reflection in the bathroom's old mirror. Her eyes were bright and her skin looked healthy. She looked aglow, Kat reflected wryly. And she felt far more alive than she had in such a long time.

Her relationship with Shael had been rocky for years, even before a well-meaning friend had told Kat that Shael had been seen with someone else. When Kat confronted her, Shael had admitted to what she told Kat was a one-night stand. Deep down Kat knew it had been more than that, but Shael swore it was over, that she was sorry and that it would never happen again. Kat suspected it had, although she had no proof.

Back then she'd decided to end it with Shael, but there had always been Meggie. She hadn't been prepared to hurt Meggie. So she'd stayed.

Nearly two years ago, Kat found out later, Shael had met Tori at the hospital where Shael was an ophthalmologist. Tori, a nursing sister, was on the right side of thirty and strikingly attractive in what Kat thought was a cold, untouchable sort of way.

Six months ago Shael had sent Meggie to her grandmother's for the night, then sat down with Kat and informed her their relationship was over. Kat hadn't been surprised, although she'd been devastated by the matter-of-fact, almost clinical way Shael had told her.

Shael decided the breakup would be easier if she remained in the house. Tori would move in and Kat would move out. Shael acknowledged the house was partially Kat's, and she would receive her portion of the proceeds when the house was eventually sold. When Kat asked when this was likely to be, Shael suggested in a couple of years, when Megghan was to attend high school.

And what, Kat had asked derisively, was she to do in the meantime? Live in the street, perhaps? Shael had angrily reminded Kat she had inherited her old girlfriend's house.

Kat had moved out a week later, and it had been a week of alternating arguments and heavy silences. Kat's heart ached, not only for herself, but for Meggie, who didn't take the breakup well. Why did it have to be this way, Meggie had asked, sobbing on Kat's shoulder, when she loved them both?

The trauma of it all had sent Kat spiraling down into a depression. Yet now, after such a short time here in this house, something positive had happened. She had found a new and positive outlook on life. The physical work was making her fitter and the fact that she was quite capable of doing the work bolstered her self-esteem. She was feeling far more like the old Kat, and that pleased her the most.

And it was all due to Jess Andrews. Kat frowned. No, Jess may have been a sort of catalyst, but Kat knew she would have felt the way she did even if she hadn't met Jess. She gave her reflection a mocking smile. Jess was just a bonus.

It was a nice change to meet someone like Jess, always pleasant, with her wonderful smile, and it certainly didn't hurt that she was especially pleasing to look at. Kat laughed out loud at herself. Could she be turning into a dirty old woman leering after a pretty young thing.

Maybe Em had been right. She needed to get out, indulge in some meaningless sex, no strings attached. Yeah right! That hadn't even been an option when she was young and foolish. She'd never gone looking for that scene. And a little voice inside her wondered if she ever had the chance. Her six-year affair with Ruth had begun when Kat was barely eighteen. And after Ruth left her for another bright young thing, she'd fallen in love with Shael a year later. She'd never been simply single for very long.

She shoved that disquieting thought out of her mind. In all honesty, living with Shael these past years she might as well have been single. Their lovemaking had been sporadic at best. Shael had a demanding and stressful job and more often than not she was too tired for more than an occasional kiss.

Yes, now that Kat was definitely single she should sow the wild oats she'd never had the chance to sow. Wild oats? Meaningless sex? No strings attached? Kat gave a skeptical laugh. She wasn't at all sure she would be able to pull that off even if she wanted to. She doubted she could voice the intention, let alone carry out the deeds.

She shook her head ruefully, knowing she hadn't exactly made such a brilliant start. Here she was all a-quiver over a straight woman.

Another bad choice? There was that same annoying little voice inside her again. Kat expelled an irritated breath. Would she recognize a good choice if it came up and bit her? She pushed all thoughts about choices out of her mind. At the moment, with Jess due to arrive, Kat didn't care to think about choices, good or bad. She simply wanted to relax and enjoy Jess's company. What harm could there be in that?

She gave her hair another vigorous brushing, only to drop her brush when she started at the knock on the front door. She quickly retrieved her brush and set it on the vanity basin. Taking a steadying breath she hurried to the door. She swung it open and couldn't prevent her smile from fading just a little. "Oh. Lucas. Hello." Her eyes moved past him, looking for Jess.

Lucas gave a rueful smile. "One and the same."

Kat stepped back, inviting him in.

"Jess had to collect the kids and take Caleb to the dentist

because he fell over and chipped a tooth. I'm a bigger wuss than the kids are at the dentist so I've been dispatched with the contracts. Sorry."

Kat recovered herself. "Oh. No. That's all right. Come into the kitchen. We can use the bench as a desk."

Lucas went through the contract and payment schedules with her, and they signed the tagged places Jess had marked.

Kat opened her chequebook. "And I guess you want a deposit."

Lucas grinned. "That would be much appreciated. Jess tells me you inherited this place," Lucas said as Kat wrote out the cheque.

Kat murmured a reply as she gave her chequebook her full attention. "That's right. From a friend."

"I knew Ruth Dunleavy," Lucas said and Kat looked up in surprise. "She was one of my tutors at University."

"She was? What year was that?"

They established that Lucas was a year behind Kat.

"We might have passed in the hallways," Lucas laughed.

"Yes. What were you studying?"

Lucas gave a crooked smile. "I have a business degree."

Kat raised her eyebrows.

"Didn't care for it though. I've always liked working with timber so I became a relatively mature-age apprentice carpenter to Mark's dad." He raised his hands and let them fall. "And I've never looked back."

"I guess your business degree must come in handy with the company," Kat said.

"Jess has a business degree as well, and she's really into that stuff. Fortunately. Mark and I usually leave all that to her. She's a whiz at it and on top of that, she has the organizational skills of a sergeant-major. That's very imperative with me and Mark because we can both be a bit lax in that department. But I can assure you," he added quickly, "we're both master tradesmen."

Kat smiled. "I know you are. Jess showed me photos of your work. Very impressive."

"We strive for perfection," he said, and Kat sensed he was completely serious. "And personally," he continued, "I can't wait to get started on this beauty." He put his hands on his hips and looked around.

Kat asked him about the sections that had priority that she was responsible for, and they walked through the house looking at what she'd done so far.

"I'll send over our sparky to stop off the electrical points and lights out here on the veranda in case it rains. Don't want the water blowing in and getting into the electrics."

Kat thanked him. "I was going to check the yellow pages for an electrician."

"Leave it to us." He took out a notebook and made a note of it.

He indicated the notebook. "Jess makes us keep a record of everything so we don't double up and so we don't make promises we don't keep." He laughed. "She's a tiger about that." He walked over and looked at the one remaining weather board in the section.

"I had to leave that one," Kat said ruefully. "The nails are stubborn and by the time I got to it my arms felt like rubber. I started to swear at it then decided to leave it till I was fresher."

"Okay if I have a go at it?" Lucas asked.

"Be my guest." Kat laughed. "I am so over that particular board."

Lucas looked around for Kat's discarded tools, and in no time the board was off and stacked on the pile.

Kat thanked him.

"No trouble. You've done really well with it, especially doing it on your own." He raised an enquiring eyebrow. "No boyfriend to give you a hand?"

Kat felt a pique of irritation. Why did men always think a woman needed a man to do everything? Even if Lucas did get that board off, Kat was confident she'd have managed the next day. She sighed inwardly and acknowledged she should just accept the help in the manner it was given.

"No. No boyfriend, partner or husband," she said as casually as she could. "I'm on my own now."

"Now? Well, that's the guy's loss."

Kat had to laugh then. "Oh, yes. I'm sure every guy wants me to work him into the ground demolishing part of a house."

Lucas laughed too. "I take your point. How long have you been on your own?"

"Officially, six months. Should have been longer." Kat wondered at Lucas's interest. She still thought he was gay. If that was so, what interest did he have in Kat's lovelife? Maybe she should put the ball in his court, so to speak. "Are you married?" she heard herself ask him.

"Me? No."

"Haven't met Ms. Right?"

"Guess not." Lucas grimaced, and his eyes met Kat's for long moments. An expression Kat couldn't fathom flickered there before Lucas turned to replace Kat's tools where he'd found them. He glanced at his wristwatch. "Well, I'd better get the contracts back to the office."

Kat walked to the door with him.

"Jess will be in touch as soon as the plans come through."

Kat watched him stride down to his car, and she wondered what that conversation had been all about—especially the unspoken one.

After Lucas left Kat drove over to Shael's house, the house that used to be her house as well, to find Meggie sitting on the front steps waiting for her. As Kat pulled to a stop in the driveway Meggie leaned inside the open door and grabbed her backpack. She called something over her shoulder and raced down the steps, heading for Kat as fast as she could.

"Hi, Kitty Kat!" She gave a little skip. "I've been ready for ages."

Shael came to the door as Meggie scrambled into the passenger seat of Kat's car and reached across to give Kat a fierce hug. They waited as Shael approached. Kat wound down her window and greeted the other woman warily.

"I'll phone you when I get back from Sydney on Monday evening," Shael said, and Kat felt a moment of regret that they had come to this cold formality. "Megghan has my mobile number in her phone if you need to contact me."

"Okay." Kat shifted the drive into reverse.

"Kat."

Kat paused and looked at Shael.

"Oh, nothing. Thanks." She stepped back. "Have a good time, Megghan. I'll see you on Tuesday."

"Yep. 'Bye, Mum." Megghan waved, and Kat reversed out onto the road.

They spent the evening watching back-to-back episodes of *Stargate SG1* and Kat fell asleep with a smile on her face, knowing she had a whole long weekend to spend with her daughter.

"Kat, come and look. They're playing cricket in the park across the road."

Kat joined Megghan out on the partially demolished veranda. She took the opportunity to brush the young girl's dark hair back from her face. Megghan leaned into Kat and Kat enveloped her in a hug. She was so happy to have some time with the ten-year-old she had to fight back tears.

"They play sports in the park every weekend," Kat told Megghan as they stood in the front doorway watching what they could see of the cricket game through the trees.

"Can we go over there and watch?" Meggie asked as she craned to see a batsman hit a six. "And did I tell you at school I'm on the girls' under-twelve cricket team?"

"No, you didn't tell me. Congratulations. I'll have to come and watch you play."

"That would be awesome. So can we go over and watch?" Meggie persisted.

"Sure. There's always a couple of games being played at one time, and there's a seating stand over on the other side of the park. I think they play the women's matches over there so we can walk over and watch them."

"Great. Let's get changed. What will we wear?" Meggie skipped inside and looked through her clothes. "I think I'll wear the new white shorts Mum bought me and this blue shirt you bought me. What do you think, Kat?"

"Perfect. And I'm opting for my denim shorts and this lemon T-shirt." Kat held up the shirt. "Now for a quick shower. Want to go first?"

Half an hour later they followed the path across the small park in front of the larger area that contained a number of ovals. To the left was a team of white-clad youths while to the right young girls had taken to the field.

They made their way to the seating section, and Kat scanned the stand for two empty seats.

"Kat! Over here!"

Kat turned at the sound of the welcoming voice to see Jess walking towards her, and she smiled and waved, experiencing that now familiar feeling in the pit of her stomach—a heady mixture of pleasure, excitement and arousal. She was just thankful that Jess was unaware of the reaction she always seemed to evoke in Kat.

"You like cricket?" Jess asked. "Or in this case, junior women's cricket."

"I've seen a bit on Fox Sport, but it's a highly ignored women's sport, isn't it? Who would watch women's cricket when they can watch men play?" she added dryly.

"Exactly. Sexism personified." Jess grimaced. "All that aside, we have a pretty good comp going. Our team's second at the moment. And this is our junior team batting. We're playing the Waratahs." She grimaced again. "Not too hopeful of getting a win this week, though, as we're down three members of the team, one with a broken arm and two sisters who are away on holidays."

"That's bad luck," Kat began.

"I can play," said a bright voice beside Kat.

"Oh." Kat put her hand on Meggie's shoulder. "Jess, meet Megghan Smith, the daughter of a friend. She's staying with me for the weekend."

"Hi! Megghan. Nice to meet you." Jess smiled and Meggie smiled back.

"You can call me Meggie for short."

Kat knew she should correct Meggie but she hadn't the heart. Much to Shael's disgust Kat had always shortened Megghan's name, while Shael always used Meggie's full name.

"Well, thank you. And I'm Jess, short for Jessica. So I take it you've played cricket before, Meggie?" Jess asked.

"Sure." Meggie shrugged. "I play at school. I'm a medium-fast bowler, and I bat at number four on our team."

"Amazing. Tell me you're under twelve," Jess said excitedly.

"I'm ten."

"I have a daughter who's ten. That's her batting now." Jess looked at Kat. "Will you give your permission for Meggie to play?"

"Well, it would be okay if it was up to me but I'm not her mother."

"Can you reach her mother?"

"I can phone her." Meggie fumbled in her backpack and brought out a bright pink mobile phone. "Mum got it for me for emergencies," she added when Kat raised her eyebrows. "Mum said I could ring her anytime so I'll ring her now." Meggie began to scroll down to Shael's number.

"I think perhaps I should speak to her," Jess began and Kat nodded reluctantly.

Shael answered right away and Meggie excitedly explained the situation before passing the phone to Jess.

Kat could only stand by and listen as Jess spoke easily to Shael. In no time at all she had signed Meggie's consent form in lieu of Shael and they had another form for Shael to sign later.

"This is so awesome," Meggie said as they sat in the stands after the game, waiting until Jess had organized rides home for a few of the girls. "And I really like Miranda. Do you know she said my score really helped the team win the game." Meggie proudly ran her hand over the team T-shirt Jess had found for her. "And Jess said I could keep the shirt and play on the team when I'm here."

"That's nice of her," Kat said, watching Jess in action as team coach.

"I could play every weekend if I like. And Jess said I could because they're always short of players," Meggie said. "I'd really like to."

Kat looked back at the child. "Well, that's up to your mother."

"But you could come over and get me, couldn't you?" she appealed.

"Let's wait until we can discuss it with your mother."

"I guess. But Kat, it would mean I'd get to see you more often." Meggie slipped her arm through Kat's and leaned against her. "That would be so cool, wouldn't it?"

Jess and Miranda joined them before Kat could reply. "Sorry to take so long, but we seem to have been at sixes and sevens this weekend." She turned to Meggie. "And thanks once again for coming to our rescue, Meggie."

"That's okay." Meggie blushed with pleasure and leaned closer to Kat.

"We'll have to thank your mother again." Jess looked at Kat. "And thanks to you too, Kat, for bringing Meggie over."

"Oh, that was Meggie's idea."

"Well, if you're not doing anything this evening we're having a fundraising barbecue right here at the clubhouse. You're both welcome. Oh, and Meggie's mother as well, of course."

"Mum's in Sydney. She needed a break. She's been working too hard."

"I see." Jess slid a glance at Kat.

"Dad and Uncle Lucas are cooking so it will be yummy," Miranda said. "Uncle Lucas is the most fabulous cook. Oh, and Dad is too."

Jess shrugged. "He is that. If we depended on me we'd be in dire straits."

"Kat's a great cook too. Better than Mum or Tori," said Meggie and Kat laughed.

"More like adequate, love," she said, hoping Meggie's mention of Shael's new partner had slipped by Jess.

"We have to have special food for my brother Caleb," Miranda continued. "He's a celiac so he can't eat wheat and stuff."

"Does it make him sick? Maybe Mum could fix him up. She's

a doctor. She mainly fixes eyes, but she knows about other doctor stuff," Meggie said helpfully.

"Thank you," Jess said with amusement. "But Caleb's fine as long as we watch what he eats."

"Does your brother play cricket too?" Meggie asked.

Miranda shook her head. "Caleb doesn't like cricket. Dad's taken him to his music lessons. My brother's very musical."

"I wish I had a brother," Meggie said wistfully. "I've been asking Mum and Kat for years and years for us to have a baby."

Kat tensed and glanced quickly at Jess to see if she'd noticed that Meggie had put Shael and Kat together. But Jess simply gave Kat a quick smile.

"Maybe you should ask your Dad," Miranda suggested, but before she could continue her mother stepped in.

"This morning Miranda didn't think having a little brother was such a good thing," Jess raised her eyebrows at her daughter, "if you recall, hmmm?"

"Oh, Mum! He was driving me bananas!" Miranda appealed and Jess gave her daughter a hug.

"I know." She turned to Kat. "Eventually we sorted it all out. With Dad's help."

"My dad builds houses. What does your dad do, Meggie?" Miranda asked and Kat stiffened.

"I don't have a father," Meggie said easily, and Miranda gave her a sympathetic look.

"Did he die?" she asked worriedly.

"Oh, no. At least I don't think so," replied Meggie. "I never knew him. Mum wasn't married to him. He was just a friend who—"

Kat gave her arm a warning squeeze and Meggie paused.

"I guess I shouldn't talk about it," she finished conspiratorily. "But I have two mothers really, Mum and Kat." She smiled up at Kat and Kat could only smile back.

"There's this boy in our class, well, he has two mothers too. And then there's Jeremy and he's got two dads." Miranda shrugged. "We just about have two dads as well. There's Dad, our real dad, and then there's Uncle Lucas and there's Mum."

"Hi, girls!"

They all turned around to see Mark Andrews approaching. With Mark was a slight fair-haired boy who bore a striking resemblance to Jess and her cousin, Lucas.

And a very propitious arrival too, Kat reflected, considering the direction of the conversation. Who knew where it would have ended with the two young girls exchanging information.

"That's my dad. And Caleb," Miranda told Meggie.

"Wow!" Meggie breathed out noisily. "Your dad is really cool looking."

"He's okay, I guess," said Miranda casually. "Hi Dad! Come and meet Kat and Meggie. Meggie played cricket with us."

"Hello again, Kat. And this devastatingly attractive young lady must be your daughter." Mark had turned his winsome smile on Meggie and she wasn't unmoved. She blushed.

"Well, Kat's almost my mother. Sort of like my other mother."

"I'm a friend of Meggie's mother," Kat put in.

"Ah. I see by your T-shirt you must be joining Miranda's team? They could use a few extra players."

"I want to but I have to ask Mum." Meggie sighed theatrically.

"And this is Caleb." Miranda introduced her brother, giving him a big sister look that went from pride to dire warning not to embarrass her.

The young boy smiled up at Kat with Jess's smile and won her immediately.

"Did Jess tell you about the barbecue tonight?" Mark asked. "We'll have the best sausages in town, and I have it on good authority that the dessert tonight will be absolutely irresistible." He sang the last bit and the children all laughed.

"Not bad," Kat complimented him and Jess shook her head. "Don't encourage him, Kat. He's the biggest ham."

"That was only to whet your appetite, Kat." Mark good-naturedly pulled a face at his ex-wife. "I'm saving my impersonation of Elvis for the barbecue."

Miranda groaned. "Oh, Dad, don't! You can be *so embarrassing*."

"I think he's really good at it," Caleb supported his father.

"See. Caleb knows a star when he sees one, don't you, mate?"

Mark ruffled his son's fair hair. He turned to Jess. "Didn't your mother say she'd have lunch ready at one? We'd better get organized if we don't want to be late."

Jess looked at her watch. "You take the kids home for a shower, and I'll just check the girls have put all the gear away."

Mark said goodbye to Kat and went off with the two children, Miranda still turning to wave at Meggie until she'd climbed into her father's car.

"Can we help with the gear?" Kat asked Jess.

"No. But thanks. There's hardly anything left to do. I just thought I'd get rid of Mark before he did any more entertaining." She laughed. "He has a penchant for Willie Nelson and Julio Iglesias."

Kat raised her eyebrows.

"I know. How's that for versatility?" Jess laughed. "Actually, he's really quite good when he gets going, but here in the middle of the park, with cricket matches going on all around, well, impersonating Elvis can be a trifle showy, even for Mark." She picked up a discarded cricket bat. "Miranda gets embarrassed and he teases her with it. Honestly those two are so alike, sometimes I could trade them both in on different models."

Kat chuckled. "Never a dull moment, hmm?"

"Exactly. So, do you think you'd like to come to the barbecue tonight?" Jess's clear blue eyes met and held Kat's. "I'd really like you to come," she said, her voice huskily sincere.

Time seemed to stand still for Kat. The trees, the sounds of birds, the thump of a cricket ball on a bat, the cheers of the onlookers all faded into the distant background and there was only Jess. Bright and bubbly, so very sexy Jess. And a Jess who had been married, reminded the voice of reason inside her. The world righted itself. She was foolishly allowing herself to be drawn into the web of Jess Andrews' attraction.

"Can we, Kat?" Meggie's voice brought her tortured thoughts back to reality as she took hold of Kat's arm.

"Well—"

"Please, Kat. It'll be fun. I like Miranda and the other girls in the team."

Kat shrugged. "Okay. What time does it start?" she asked Jess.

"Six o'clock. And we'll set up a couple of extra folding chairs at our table for you. See you then."

Just before six Kat and Meggie headed back across the park to the cricket clubhouse. Foldout tables and chairs had been set out beside the clubhouse under the trees, and the trees glowed with brightly colored strung lights. A small band was playing, and a few people were already dancing on a flat grass-covered area in front of the clubhouse.

The enticing smell of sausages and onions on the barbecue wafted on the air and Kat realized she was hungry. Since she'd made the break to move into Ruth's house her appetite was slowly returning. Tonight, with the aroma of the sausage sizzle, her tummy rumbled, she suspected her appetite had turned up and brought along a group of friends.

The Andrews family was sitting at a large table, and Jess stood up with a smile as they approached. In no time Kat was sitting across from Jess while Meggie and Miranda were talking and laughing together.

Lucas joined them bringing a tray full of crusty bread rolls filled with sausage and grilled onions and topped with sauce and mustard to pass around. Kat took a bite of her roll and murmured appreciatively. When she'd finished her roll she looked up to see Jess watching her as she licked her fingers. Embarrassed, she searched for a napkin.

Jess laughed as she handed Kat a paper towel. "Does that mean you enjoyed it?"

"Mmm. Delicious."

"Would you like another one?"

"Oh, no. Thanks." Kat patted her stomach. "I'm full. But it was fantastic."

"I hope you've saved a small space because we have special homemade ice cream for dessert. The mother of one of the players makes it herself. I think we have two choices, blueberry or mango."

Kat groaned.

"Kat always says she'll do anything for ice cream," put in Meggie and Jess wiggled her eyebrows.

"Anything?" she asked.

Kat shook her head and heat rose in her body. "Well, almost anything," she said huskily, and she saw Jess look quickly away. Was she imagining the underlying awareness she'd seen in Jess's eyes or was she simply seeing something she wanted to see. No, she hadn't imagined it, she told herself, and her mouth went dry. She took a sip of her soft drink and tried to concentrate on the conversation around her.

Fortunately at that moment Meggie asked Kat to dance with her, and Kat gratefully left the table and went onto the dance floor. A short time later Jess and Miranda joined them. Somehow they changed partners and Meggie and Miranda danced together and Kat was left facing Jess as they moved to the music. At least there was no touching with these dances, Kat reflected. But she still got to watch Jess, the way she moved, the way the artificial light flickered in her fair hair, accentuated the planes and angles of her lovely face and her slow, sexy smile.

Tonight Jess was wearing white jeans and a dark blue top, the scalloped neckline resting on the swell of her breasts. Kat thought she looked absolutely fantastic. So why would her husband want to divorce her?

Kat slid a glance at the handsome Mark Andrews. He was cleaning the barbecue, laughing at something Lucas was saying. With his compelling looks, Kat could understand if he was a womanizer, but he didn't seem to be at all like that. He seemed pleasant to both men and women. In Kat's experience some men couldn't seem to help themselves running their eyes over women in a particularly irritating, almost predatory way. When Kat had met Mark Andrews in the office he hadn't given her any of the usual bad vibes.

Perhaps Jess had strayed? Kat looked back at Jess. She was attractive, vivacious, all that her husband was. And just like Mark, she was simply nice to everyone, not singling anyone out.

Suddenly Kat realized she'd been staring at Jess and Jess was watching her. They gazed at each other for long tension-filled moments, then Kat gave a nervous laugh. "You're a great dancer."

Jess's smile was a little forced. "Do you reckon? Something tells me you don't get out much, Kat."

Kat laughed spontaneously. "You should be a detective. It's been so long since I danced sure as eggs I'll be stiff as a board tomorrow. But I still say you're a great dancer."

"Then, thanks." Jess inclined her head. "Want to sit down before I blot my copybook?"

"Sure." Kat followed Jess back to the table, knowing she could keep an eye on Meggie from there.

"Phew!" Jess wiped her forehead with a tissue. "I think I'm with you, Kat. I need to go to the gym."

"No, you don't, Mum," said Caleb sleepily. "You're beautiful."

Jess gave him a hug as Kat reflected she thoroughly agreed with the eight-year-old. She looked back to see Meggie and Miranda walking towards them, accompanied by another child about their own age.

"Look, Mum," said Miranda. "Katie's arm's all better. She gets her plaster off on Monday so she'll be able to play again soon."

"Look at my arm, Jess. Everyone's signed it for me."

Jess dutifully admired the young girl's colorfully autographed plaster cast before introducing her to Kat. "This is Katie Farrelly. Katie's one of the wounded members of the team."

"Hi, Katie. Is this cricket a dangerous game then?" Kat asked with mock seriousness.

Katie laughed. "Not really, Mrs. Oldfield. I actually fell off my bike. I came flying down the road to my mum's gardening centre, and I hit a bit of gravel that had dropped off a truck. I flew way up in the air and landed on my arm," she finished with relish.

"And your mother tells me you were a very lucky young lady," Jess said.

"More than lucky," stated a tall dark-haired woman who walked up and rested her hands on Katie's shoulders.

"Oh, Mum. I told you. I actually jumped off the bike, then I tripped over the gutter." Katie rolled her eyes.

Jess laughed. "How are you, Quinn?" she asked Katie's mother. "Is Rachel here?"

Quinn looked around. "Over talking to Mark. She's probably telling him how Adam kicked the winning goal in his soccer game this afternoon."

Jess made the introductions. "Kat, meet Quinn Farrelly, one of the owners of the best landscaping business around here. If you're looking to get your garden redesigned then Rachel and Quinn are the ones to call. R&R Gardening and Landscaping is the most fantastic place for gardening needs."

"I'll have to come and talk to you when I've finished renovating," Kat said as another woman joined them.

The woman brushed Quinn's arm, standing close to her, and they exchanged a glance that had Kat's gaydar clanging.

"Great timing, Rachel," Jess said. "Come and meet Kat Oldfield. Kat, this is Rachel Weston. Rachel's the other half of R&R Gardening and Landscaping," Jess explained and Kat shook hands with the woman.

The two women joined them, sitting close together, and Kat decided they were definitely a couple. Their whole demeanor said togetherness. But it was the way they looked at each other that sealed it. Love shone through every look, every touch.

Kat swallowed a sudden lump in her throat. She really envied them. How she wished she wasn't the harbinger of death for relationships. She forced the depressing thought away and tried to concentrate on the conversation around her.

They all sat chatting easily and, apart from her moment of wistfulness, Kat realized she was really enjoying the evening. She relaxed, acknowledging she had missed the company of friends. Even though her isolation was mostly self-imposed she had discovered her friends seemed to have been Shael's friends. With a sense of betrayal this had sent Kat further into herself. Had she not had her job and Em's friendship she suspected she would have slipped into a deeper depression.

And there was Meggie. Kat knew the young girl had been devastated when Shael and Kat broke up. Even though they had both been quick to assure Meggie that the breakup had not been Meggie's fault, Meggie's main concern was the fact that she was unable to see Kat daily. It was Kat's worry, too, and she and Shael had still not sorted that out. They were due to go to mediation next month.

"Kat?" Jess's voice brought Kat back to the present.

"Oh, sorry! Guess I was miles away."

"It's just last call for drinks. We wondered if you wanted something. A beer? Another Bundy Dark and Stormy? Or coffee?"

Kat shook her head. "No. But thanks. If I have caffeine this late at night it's not pretty, and another beverage of an alcoholic nature would have me needing assistance going back across the park."

"Our daughter Fliss is the same with caffeine," said Quinn. "She gets mega-hyper."

They discussed caffeine horror stories for a while, then Rachel turned to Kat with a slight frown.

"Before, did you mean you were going to walk across the park tonight?"

"Well, yes. Meggie and I walked over. I've just moved into a house on the other side of the park," Kat explained. "And I've just started renovating it."

"Ah." Rachel nodded. "You mean the Dunleavy house? Where Betty and Tess lived? I noticed when I drove by a few days ago it was having some work done on it. Next door to Grace and Tom Worrall."

"Yes. That's it."

Kat caught Rachel exchanging a quick glance with Quinn.

"So you own the house?" Rachel asked casually. "What do you plan on doing with it?"

"I wasn't planning much in the beginning but, well, it's turned into a fairly major job. In fact, I've just signed up with Handy Andrews for the construction work."

"That's a good move," Rachel said sincerely. "They're the best in the business."

"Thanks for that," Jess said, pleased.

"No worries. It's the truth. That place of yours has so much potential, Kat, doesn't it?"

"We all agree on that," Jess said. "And Lucas thinks there's the original pressed metal ceilings under the lowered ceilings in the living room."

"That's great," said Quinn. "Rachel and I would love to come and see it some time, wouldn't we, Rach? If it's okay with you, Kat."

"Of course."

"I hope you're taking before and after photos," said Rachel. "If not, I'm sure Jess will. She loves doing that. They have a marvelous collection of photos of the properties they've worked on."

"I have taken some photos," Kat told them. "And I planned on recording every stage once Jess starts the actual renovations."

"Jess?" Quinn put on a horrified face. "You don't plan on letting Jess near an electric saw, do you, Kat?"

Jess gave her a playful shove. "Ha! Ha! You know very well I'm the finance department."

"Now stop teasing Jess, Quinn," chastised Rachel.

"Yes, stop teasing me, you bully, Quinn Farrelly."

They all laughed and Rachel turned to Kat.

"It's a bit of a long-standing joke, you see, Kat. The first time Jess tried to use an electric saw, besides cutting her piece of timber, she cut through the stand she was working on, which just happened to be Mark's father's favorite sawhorse. Since then they've banned her from using power tools."

"It was just a small accident," Jess justified.

"And then there was the time with the electric drill," Quinn began.

"Stop it, Quinn." Jess appealed. "You'll be making Kat start looking for loopholes to get out of the contract we've just signed."

Quinn waved her hand. "No problems, Kat. By law you have a ten-day cooling off period for cases such as this. Luckily, it's not too late."

Jess turned an imploring gaze on Kat. "Don't listen to her, Kat. I promise I won't be doing any of the hands-on work on your house. I'm strictly in charge of the cash flow."

Kat was still trying to settle the flutters in her stomach that multiplied when Jess looked at her, but she made herself laugh.

"On every job site," Quinn continued, obviously on a roll, "they have one of those danger signs with the red circle and the line through it, over a picture of Jess holding a drill."

Rachel took Quinn to task as they all dissolved into laughter again. When they'd recovered they realized most people had left or were leaving.

"Heavens! Look at the time," Kat remarked. "We should be getting off home too."

Rachel groaned. "And so much for our early night. Must be the fantastic company."

"I agree. It's been a great night," said Quinn. "And if you want to try your hand at cricket yourself, Kat, you're welcome on our team anytime."

Kat laughed. "You don't know what you're saying. I'm perfect as a spectator."

"Well, we need those too." Quinn touched Kat's arm and turned back to Jess. "We should finish off the property in Crane Street tomorrow as long as the forecasted rain holds off. Ken got all the machinery out this afternoon so the driveway can be paved."

Jess rolled her eyes. "I'm only surprised the rain has held off long enough for us to finish. Now there's a renovation, Kat. The house is clinging to the side of Mt. Coot-tha, and it's been a nightmare getting everything onto the site."

"But the views are spectacular," added Rachel.

"So you've been working together on the property," said Kat.

"Yes." Jess nodded. "We did the renovations and Rachel and Quinn are just finishing off the landscaping. The owners are overjoyed by the results. These two know their business."

Rachel and Quinn grinned. "We love it when the customers want an easy-care, water-wise, natural Aussie garden," said Rachel. "And in this case it fits in magnificently with the setting and the house."

Quinn checked her wristwatch too, and sighed. "And if I'm going to get out there early we'd better head off. Ready, kids?"

Rachel smiled at Kat as she stood up. "It was so nice to meet you and Meggie."

Kat watched them walk away, noting the hand Quinn laid on Rachel's back, the arm she rested around the shoulders of her daughter.

"Nice family," Jess said beside Kat.

"Yes." Kat swallowed, reflecting that Jess may be straight, but she obviously wasn't intolerant. What if Kat told her—

"Kat, are we really going to walk home across the park?" Meggie asked. "It's really dark."

Kat looked towards the path. "I brought a torch. We'll be right. It'll only take a few minutes to get home."

"No need to walk. If you can wait a while I can drop you home. I just have to give them a hand to stack away the chairs and tables."

"We can help, too," said Meggie, picking up her chair. "Where do we put them?"

With everything stowed in the clubhouse, they all piled into Jess's people mover van. Jess drove around the outskirts of the park and pulled up in front of Kat's house. Kat and Meggie thanked her and she drove away, Meggie waving to Miranda until the taillights of their van disappeared around the corner into the darkness. And Kat wanted to wave just like Meggie did.

A few mornings later, after a leisurely breakfast, Meggie suggested they catch up on the next episode of *Stargate SG-1*. They'd just started watching it when Kat's phone rang.

"I'll get it," Meggie said, dashing to pick up the phone, as Kat muted the sound on the TV. "Hello. Kat's phone." Meggie grinned. "Sure, Jess. She's here. We're watching the *Stargate* series. Have you seen it? We're up to the part where those awful Ori—"

Kat coughed loudly and shook her head when Meggie looked around, and her smile broadened.

"Oops! Sorry, Jess," she apologized. "Kat says not everyone's as wrapped in sci-fi as we are." Her face beamed with pleasure. "You do. That's great. Who's your favorite? Kat and I just love Sam Carter. Actually," Meggie's face was now all serious concentration, "you look a bit like Sam, Jess."

"Meggie!" Kat said warningly, although she secretly agreed. Jess and Samantha Carter were the same build and coloring, with similar short fair hair.

"Sorry," Meggie apologized. "I'll hand you over to Kat."

Kat took the phone. "Hello, Jess. Or should I say Major Carter?"

Jess laughed and a warm glow began inside Kat. "Don't worry. I won't ask you to salute."

"We're not quite as fanatical about *Stargate* as Meggie may have led you to believe."

"That's okay. We all like it here too. Another favorite of mine is *Star Trek Voyager*."

"Ours too," Kat agreed. "Strong female lead and a fantastic story about the basic emotive need to get home."

"Exactly. We'll have to watch some episodes. Mark and Lucas prefer *The Next Generation* so it would be great to watch *Voyager* with someone who enjoys it as much as Miranda and I do. But, apart from that," Jess continued as Kat dragged her imagination away from the scene where Kat and Jess sat cuddled on the couch with the *Voyager* theme playing in the background and Janeway's husky voice giving the order to set a course for home.

"We were wondering if you and Meggie had made any plans for the rest of the day."

"Plans?" Kat tried to focus on reality.

"Yes. For two reasons, actually," Jess added.

"Nothing concrete, unless you count heading off-world with *SG-1*, that is."

Jess laughed again, and the warm glow inside Kat began to blossom into a far more overwhelming fire.

"If we can we'd like to make a start on the back bathroom, and I suspect Lucas also wants to investigate under the living room ceiling. He's been talking about it ever since the day he saw it. However, the downside for you and Meggie is that it's going to be noisy and disruptive, so that leads me to part two of my proposal. I'm taking the kids for a picnic, and we thought you and Meggie might like to come along. It will get you out of the house for the initial inconvenience of marauding tradesmen. What do you say?"

Kat realized she was smiling as broadly as Meggie had been. "Sounds fantastic. Where were you planning on going and what can we bring?"

"Just bring yourselves. I have the picnic lunch under control. There's a really nice picnic area about half an hour from here so what if we pick you up in about an hour?"

Before they knew it Kat had left Lucas in charge at the house, and she was seated beside Jess in her people mover with the three children in the back, heading along an open road.

Later, Kat murmured appreciatively. "That was magnificent." She'd just helped Jess stow the remains of their picnic lunch back in its containers. "Thanks so much for asking us, Jess."

"No problem. It fitted in wonderfully with Mark and Lucas, and, of course, with the kids and me. I try to get as much time off as I can manage when the kids are on school holidays, and we love doing this sort of thing."

They sat on the sturdy wooden picnic benches watching the kids in the playground nearby. Jess filled Kat in on the timeframe for the renovation jobs, then they moved on to books they'd read and movies they'd seen. While part of Kat sat relaxing, enjoying simply being with Jess, taking in each facet of Jess and her life and basking in the opportunity to get to know her better, a small part of her desperately wanted so much more.

She wanted to touch Jess's tanned skin, kiss her wonderful lips, feel the length of Jess's body beside hers. It was an exquisite mixture of pleasure and pain. And it was something Kat knew she was going to have to curb. Deep down she recognized that in reality she couldn't keep thinking of Jess in this way. She had to accept their relationship on a friendly business footing because if Jess so much as suspected Kat felt the way she did she'd quickly, and no doubt politely, put as much distance as possible between them. If Kat wanted to continue with this growing friendship with Jess she'd have to banish these feelings to the far reaches of her mind. If she was capable of doing just that, she reminded herself.

"You look like you were having a doze with your eyes open." Jess's words brought Kat out of her troubled thoughts.

"I was I guess. Drifting after the delicious meal, in such beautiful weather, with very enjoyable company." Kat stifled a yawn. "Sorry. That's the result of the food and the weather and not the company, I assure you."

"I'll have to take your word for that." Jess grinned at her.

"Promise. I was just thinking about the renovations." Kat resisted the urge to cross her fingers as she stretched the truth.

"You'll be surprised how quickly it will progress," Jess told her. "We're very experienced at organizing everything, dovetailing the work, the various tradesmen involved. I do that while Mark and Lucas handle all the hands-on details. We're a good team. Just settle back and enjoy the ride."

The children ran up then and they had fresh fruit for dessert. They spent the afternoon walking the paths in the park and playing Frisbee. Kat felt exhausted but mellow by the time Jess dropped them at home. Kat watched her drive away with genuine regret that the wonderful day was over.

"Miranda and I have decided we're going to be honorary sisters," Meggie said as she settled into Kat's new bed later that night. "I've always wanted a sister. Haven't I always said that?"

"That you have." And not always at the most appropriate time either, Kat reflected, recalling one quite embarrassing Christmas at Shael's parents' house when six-year-old Meggie had brought up the subject.

"Why didn't we ever have more children, Kat?" Meggie asked. "I know you love kids." She paused. "Well, you love me. So why didn't you have a baby, too?"

"It just never fit in," Kat said. "Now, off to sleep. We've had a big day."

"Yes, but—" Meggie sighed loudly. "Oh, well. That's okay now because Miranda's going to be my sister."

Kat lay awake long after Meggie fell asleep, mulling over the past and feeling the familiar depression begin to take hold. If she and Shael hadn't allowed their relationship to wither and die would Shael have eventually agreed to Kat having a child? Kat knew the answer would be no. The arguments they'd had swirled around inside her until she was restless and agitated.

No. No more of the past. She'd concentrate on the wonderful

day they'd shared with Jess and her children. And she drifted off to sleep with a smile on her face and Jess filling her thoughts.

The construction work went on full steam ahead and Kat was impressed. So that the tradesmen had no interruptions Kat and Meggie made themselves scarce, going Christmas shopping even though Christmas was a month away and bicycle riding in the park across the street. They even took a drive to the coast and back. Meggie begged Kat to ask Jess, Miranda and Caleb to go with them, but Jess was working so Kat took all three children for a swim in the surf. Her one regret was that Jess was out of the office when she dropped the children back. However, Mark thanked her and reminded her the kitchen would be installed the next day.

Kat was looking in her refrigerator trying to decide what to have for dinner when she heard light footfalls on the front steps. Her body tensed, her nerve endings shifting into overdrive when she heard Jess's husky voice.

"Hi, Kat. Are you accepting uninvited visitors?"

Kat closed the fridge door and strode around the breakfast bar into the living room. Jess wasn't wearing her usual uniform of tailored shorts and shirt. Instead she had on neat jeans with a white collared shirt under a darkish blue jacket.

"Sure," she said, quickly suspecting she'd accept Jess anytime anywhere. "Come on in and sit down. You're working late tonight."

"I feel like I've been working for days." Jess sat in one of the lounge chairs and expelled a breath of relief. "I mean, for days and nights. Oh," she waved her hand, "you know what I mean."

"That I do. Got time for a cuppa?"

"I'd love one." Jess looked up. "But only if you're having one."

"Jug's ready to boil." Kat went to move back to the kitchen. "Did I mention I love the revamped kitchen?"

Jess stood up, followed her into the kitchen and nodded. "Lucas told me you were pleased when he showed me the after photos. I knew you'd like it. It came up really well and makes the world of difference."

"Grace popped in yesterday, and she gives it her nod of approval too."

Jess smiled. "All good then."

Kat reached for the teabags. With Jess standing beside her suddenly the perfectly adequate-sized kitchen had become far too small. "Actually, I was just thinking of dinner and a toasted cheese and tomato sandwich. Are you hungry?"

Jess hesitated.

"It's okay if you're not. I mean, I guess you have to get home to the family."

"No, it's not that. As a matter of fact Mark and Lucas have taken the kids roller-skating. They're getting a meal there. I was supposed to go, but after the day I've had I couldn't find the energy. So I told them to go without me. I was going to grab a takeaway on the way home."

Kat shrugged. "You're welcome to chance my culinary skills. I could cook us something?"

"Actually, I had a big lunch, a business lunch, so the toasted sandwich sounds divine. If it's not putting you to too much trouble."

"No trouble. I was going to make one for myself anyway." Kat watched Jess running her hand over the finish on the countertop.

"Can I do anything to help you?" Jess asked.

"No. Just relax. I'll have it a-toasting in no time." Kat started putting out the ingredients. She relaxed a little when Jess returned to the living room.

"You know, this is a very comfy chair." Jess wriggled and settled back with an appreciative sigh.

"It's had many years of backsides molding it into submission, that's for sure."

Jess made no comment, and when Kat looked up from slicing tomatoes she saw Jess rest her cheek on her hand and close her eyes. Kat watched her, the line of her jaw, the small perfect nose, the half circle of eyelashes resting on her cheek. A strand of fair hair flopped forward over her brow, and Kat wanted to go over and brush it gently back behind her ear the way she'd seen Jess do herself so many times.

With their sandwiches in the griller, Kat quietly got out plates and cutlery. She set the kettle boiling and took down a couple of mugs and added the teabags. The click of the kettle shutting off seemed to reverberate loudly and Kat flinched, glancing over to see Jess's eyes open.

"Sorry," she said ruefully. "All sounds echo loudly in here."

Horrified, Jess pushed herself to her feet. "I'm the one who should be sorry for being so rude."

"You weren't rude, just tired," Kat said quickly.

Jess stretched, her jacket falling open, her silky white shirt molding the curve of her breasts, and Kat felt a wave of heat rush over her. Her nerve endings tingled as a torrent of wanting surged within her. Her fingers fumbled and she dropped the teaspoons in the sink with a noisy clatter. Lucky she hadn't been holding the kettle of boiling water, she told herself, and bit back a laugh.

By the time Kat had pulled herself together and looked back at Jess, the other woman was standing on the other side of the breakfast bar, far too close—and far too far away.

"I didn't mean to drop off," Jess was saying. "I don't usually. But I have had a hectic few days at work. Then the dog decided to be sick last night so it was off to the after-hours vet at midnight."

"Was he all right?" Kat asked, making their tea.

"Fine now. After much money changed hands and he coughed up, among other things, a perfectly good golf ball." Jess shook her head. "Honestly, that dog will eat anything that's lying around."

Kat chuckled.

"And all this was the night before I was to make a speech at one of the biggest business lunches of the year. So it was drive into the city, win over everyone in the room with my prepared business projections and eat loads too much yummy food. Actually," she held up her hand, "that part wasn't so bad. And it was after my turn at the podium so I could relax and enjoy it."

"Just as long as you don't expect my toasted sandwich to stack up against haute cuisine." Kat cut the sandwiches and put them on the plates.

"After what I ate at lunch I shouldn't be having anything, but they smell delicious," Jess said as she took the plate from Kat.

"Sorry I don't have a dining room table. We'll have to make do with the coffee table." Kat pulled it forward and sat Jess's mug of tea where she could reach it. On her way back to the kitchen she stopped and turned back to Jess. "I never thought to ask if you would rather have a glass of wine. I have red or white."

"No, thanks. Tea's fine." Jess laughed softly. "And far safer. If I'm falling asleep in my chair already then who knows what might happen if I get into the wine."

"Hmmm," Kat murmured noncommittally, wishing she could make some witty comment about the bed not being far away. She picked up her tea and sandwich and sat down opposite Jess.

As they ate their snack Jess kept Kat entertained with amusing stories about the people at the business lunch. Kat wished she could freeze time, have Jess here with her forever. Jess of the sexy voice, the expressive eyes, the so-enticing body.

"That was as delicious as it smelled," Jess said, wiping her hands on her paper towel.

"Basic, but fills a spot," Kat agreed.

"Oh, I'm into basic. Mark and Lucas are cooking freaks and sometimes they go a bit overboard. The kids even grumble and say they just want soup and toast."

"You and Mark seem to get on pretty well," Kat heard herself say before she realized she was going to say it. "You said you'd been divorced for six years, didn't you?" she added hurriedly.

"Yes. We stuck it out for a couple of years, trying to make it work."

Kat watched Jess's face, trying to decide if there was any residual pain or distress in her expression, but she didn't seem to be anything more than regretful. She couldn't even begin to guess at the reason why Jess and Mark's marriage might fail. They were an attractive, easygoing couple who seemed to have it all. A successful business. Two great kids. "What happened?"

A fleeting expression of pain crossed Jess's face, then Kat was contrite.

"I'm sorry. I didn't mean to pry," she began.

Jess shook her head. "That's okay. It just happened." She sighed.

"Look, Jess. I really am sorry. I didn't mean to stir up old wounds." Kat made herself laugh softly. "Just tell me to mind my own business."

"No. I wouldn't do that. I don't really mind, and a lot of it's out there in the public domain, so to speak."

"Yes, but if it upsets you to talk about it—"

"It's okay, Kat. Honestly. It's just a long, long story."

"I'm a good listener if you want to talk," Kat said.

CHAPTER FIVE

Jess's blue eyes met Kat's, and that same ripple of awareness hit Kat somewhere in the vicinity of her heart. All that was in her that was vulnerable began to go on safety alert. She knew in that infinitesimal second that she was falling for Jess, and she needed to build some fairly sturdy defenses against what would very probably only cause her pain. She knew she should put a stop to this, make some excuse that she was tired and send Jess on her way before she got any more involved with her. But, of course, Kat didn't.

"Our history, Mark's and mine," Jess was saying, "goes back over twenty years. Lucas's, too," she added softly.

Kat raised her eyebrows.

"We were just kids," Jess said with a wry smile. "We lived in the same street. Mark and I, that is. Lucas didn't move in until later. Mark lived next door. He was an only child and there was just my sister, Jen, who's three years older than me, and me. It was the same old story. We grew up together. Mark and I went to school together. Lucas didn't move into the street until Mark and I were about nine or so."

"Lucas is your cousin, right?"

Jess nodded. "His mother and mine are twins."

"That would account for why you look so much alike. You could be brother and sister," Kat remarked.

"People have always thought so." Jess laughed. "But I'm always reminding Lucas he's my little brother as he's eight months younger than me." She sobered. "But our lives couldn't have been more different. You see, my parents have always had a happy marriage. They've been married for nearly forty years and care about each other, whereas Lucas's parents, well," Jess wrinkled her nose. "Lucas's parents' marriage was pretty rocky right from the start, according to my mother. She said she always suspected all wasn't well with her sister's marriage, but she didn't know how bad it was until they moved into a rented house in our street when Lucas was eight." Jess shook her head, and a strand of fair hair fell over her forehead. She absently brushed it back behind her ear, frowning at her memories. "What were your parents like?" she asked Kat and Kat grimaced.

"Not cruel but far from kind," she said as lightly as she could.

"I know how lucky Jen and I were to have the parents we did, and Mark was the same with his parents," Jess said sincerely. "Poor Lucas. His father was diabolically hard on him. I know my parents were horrified about the way he treated Lucas, but Lucas's father's excuse was that he was 'making a man of the boy' whatever that means," Jess finished bitterly. "Lucas's father would go out drinking then he'd come home and start to verbally abuse my aunt before starting on Lucas. Lucas practically lived at our place to escape it all."

"It must have been difficult for you all," Kat said.

"The three of us, Mark, Lucas and I were great friends. We

did everything together. Mark was taller than Lucas and me and no one dared to tease or bully us." She smiled.

"A bit of protection never goes astray," Kat agreed. "As a school teacher I know kids can be cruel."

Jess nodded. "Not to us with Mark around. Lucas used to call him Sir Mark of Lancelot, protector of all small and wimpy ones." She laughed. "Which was okay with the kids at school, but Mark wanted to carry it on with Lucas's father, who was a big, broad guy. Mark nearly got himself into trouble there. We were about thirteen or fourteen and there was this really memorable day." She glanced at Kat. "You know those days when it seems like everything happens at once?"

Kat nodded.

"This particular day started out with us having our first argument. Well, Mark and Lucas did. Over me, can you believe?"

Kat could, but she made no comment.

"I mean, I'd always just been one of the boys, so to speak, and they ended up arguing about who was going to marry me. My mother sent both boys home and me to my room whereupon I got the next stage of the birds and the bees lecture." Jess chuckled. "I was mortified. And then Mum suggested that perhaps I shouldn't see so much of Mark and Lucas."

"As soon as I could get away I went over to Mark's in search of them. Lucas had gone home, but I gave Mark a huge lecture of my own, ending with the fact that I wasn't going to marry either of them."

"That's telling them," Kat said.

"Exactly. Poor Mark really copped it. And then Lucas came back. We knew something was wrong with him as soon as we saw him. He looked like he'd been crying and his left eye was all swollen and bruised. It seemed when he went home his father had started in on him again and for the first time Lucas had answered him back. And his father hit him. I've never seen Mark so angry. He took off down the road with every intention of punching Lucas's father back."

"Wow! Sir Mark of Lancelot to the rescue. He didn't, though, did he?" Kat asked.

"Not for want of trying. Lucas went after Mark, and I ran and got Mark's father. It was lucky that by the time Mark got to Lucas's house Lucas's father had gone off in search of more beer so he wasn't there. Lucas's mother was at work so Mark's father herded us back to his place. My parents were called over and we had more lectures. But," Jess held up her finger, "I did get to tell Lucas I wasn't marrying him either."

"Poor Lucas. A marriage refusal on top of everything. That *was* quite a day."

Jess nodded. "Then, when Lucas was fifteen, my aunt met another man and she left Lucas's father. Not before time, that's for sure. Anyway, Lucas went to Melbourne with his mother and her boyfriend."

"And Lucas's father stayed?"

"For a time. Then he moved to a boarding house. He was killed in an accident at work when Lucas was nineteen. My aunt then married her longtime boyfriend, and Lucas came back to Brisbane to go to University. He boarded with us, and the three of us took up where we left off."

"And you married Mark."

"Mark and I had continued to go around together, and everyone just surmised we were an item." Jess shrugged. "I suppose we were an item, but I think it was just, well, habit I guess. And not long after Lucas came back Mark proposed and I accepted. It seemed the right thing to do. Our parents were happy, but they wanted us to wait a couple of years, thought we were too young. Mark had been through his carpentry apprenticeship and was working with his father. We could afford to get married so we did. He was twenty-one and I was six months younger. We had Miranda and Caleb, I finished my degree and Mark buried himself in the business."

"And it should have been happily ever after, hmmm?" Kat said softly and Jess nodded.

"Admitting to each other we'd made a mistake getting married was the right thing for both of us. It was somewhat—" Jess smiled ruefully—"traumatic for all—" She paused, slid a quick glance at Kat, and continued, "For both of us. But Mark and I had always been great friends, and after an initial readjustment we went back to being just that, good friends."

"It sounds like you've got an enviable relationship."

Jess nodded. "It works for us. And I'm truly grateful for that. I think, I hope, it's been easier on the kids." She looked across at Kat. "I'm sorry. I've been waffling on about me, me, and more me and I haven't asked about you."

"Not much to tell really. Boring in fact."

"I somehow doubt that." She leaned across and tapped Kat on the knee. "So what's the Kat Oldfield story?"

Kat's knee tingled where Jess had touched her, and a spiral of desire skittered about inside her.

"Come on, Kat," Jess encouraged with a smile. "I have to warn you I'm not leaving until you give me at least a potted version of your life."

So that's how Kat could hold her captive. If only it would work. "Well, let's see. I was born about six streets from here. My father worked in a bank. My mother in retail. I have one sister, Beth, who's much older than me. I'm a school teacher and I'm using the summer holidays to renovate this place." Kat raised her hands and let them fall. "That's about it."

"That's all."

"I warned you I was boring."

"Rubbish," Jess exclaimed. "Have you been married yourself?" she asked easily. "Or is that too personal?"

"No. I— No. Not exactly."

"Not exactly?" Jess repeated, giving Kat a questioning look.

Kat could have bitten her tongue. What had possessed her to give Jess such a lead-in. She tried to laugh, but it came out a little forced. "Sounds weird put that way, doesn't it?" She said as lightly as she could, telling herself to hurry and mend her conversational fences. "I meant I've been in two long-ish relationships but," she shrugged, "neither worked out."

"I'm sorry. That's hard." Jess looked sympathetic, and Kat felt an almost overwhelming urge to place a so soft kiss on Jess's incredible lips. "Life can be a real pain sometimes."

"That it can."

"So you're not in a relationship now?" Jess persisted.

"No, not at the moment."

"How long have you been on your own?"

"Six months or so."

"Ah," Jess murmured. "It's pretty new then."

"Quite honestly, we should have called it quits years before we did. That would have been the most sensible thing to do." And they would have had it not been for Meggie, Kat wanted to add.

"And saved a lot of stress, no doubt." Jess gave a wry smile. "But when it comes to relationships, who's sensible?"

"That about covers it."

"So what caused your breakup?"

"Same old, same old. Another woman." Kat felt on more stable ground with that comment. "What about you?"

Jess looked down at her hands. "Oh, no other woman. As I said we both just decided we didn't want to be married anymore. It was all quite amicable."

"And have you met anyone else since your divorce?" Kat was amazed at herself. It wasn't usual for her to be so, well, so much like Em. Em would be proud of her.

"No, I haven't." Jess paused. "Not really. No one special. Life can be a bit hectic for that, what with work and the kids."

"I guess so. And the good ones aren't exactly thick on the ground, are they?"

"No. Definitely not." Jess smiled again. "My mother keeps telling us—Mark, Lucas and me—that she's sure someone special will come along for the three of us. Mum's a little bit in denial. She took Mark's and my breakup pretty hard, and I think she still holds out a glimmer of hope we'll get back together again, even though we've explained we won't be. She's coming around to it all little by little."

"What about Mark's parents?"

"Initially I think they were devastated, but they're very accepting and they love the kids. Mark and I are really grateful our parents have been so tolerant."

"What about Lucas? Isn't he seeing someone?" Kat put in and Jess looked at her quickly and away again.

"Lucas doesn't talk about that sort of thing much."

"Ah." Kat nodded. "The quiet type. I keep telling Em there's nothing wrong with that when she accuses me of being the same. Nobody gets to be shy and retiring when Em's around so you'd best warn Lucas on the off-chance they cross paths."

"I'll do that." Jess gave a smile. "And somehow I got that impression when I met Em." She paused again. "I take it you've known Em a long time?"

"Yes, since we were kids. And Em's always been the same. She'd be a valuable asset to ASIO or any other government body seeking information."

Jess laughed, and the warm, husky sound flowed over Kat like warm sunshine on a hot summer's day. She pulled herself together. "But where were we?" she asked quickly. "Oh, yes. Lucas. He's very-nice looking, isn't he? It's a wonder he's not fighting off hordes of women."

"Yes, he is pretty good looking." Jess's fingers fiddled with the collar of her shirt, the lapels of her jacket.

"There's a strong family resemblance between you and Lucas," Kat continued, wondering what had unsettled Jess. "Probably because your mothers were twins."

"Probably. Let's see. You said Lucas was good looking and that we looked alike." Jess pulled a face. "So I'll take that as a compliment then?"

"Absolutely," Kat agreed, wishing she could tell Jess just how attractive she thought she was. "It goes without saying that you must also be fighting off"—she paused and felt herself color slightly—"the hordes."

Jess held up her hands. "I assure you, I'm not. And apart from that, I'm afraid I don't need those complications."

Kat's heart sank. Strike two. Not a lesbian and not interested. Oh well, what had Kat expected? Soaring violin music, white doves, fluffy white clouds and a fairy-tale happy ending? Not likely. But it would have been so very nice, said that vulnerable part of herself she'd tried to tuck away deep inside her.

Kat's mobile rang and they both started. Kat excused herself and crossed to the breakfast bar.

"It's me," said a forlorn little voice, and Kat smiled across at Jess, mouthing that it was Meggie. "Meggie, how are you?"

"Oh, okay, I guess."

"Oh. Just okay you guess?"

"Mum's taking me over to Gran's tomorrow for the rest of the week, and I'd rather be with you."

"You like staying with your grandparents and they'd be upset if you didn't. You know how much your Gran looks forward to the school holidays so you can stay with them," Kat reminded her.

"I know. But it's Caleb's birthday and Miranda wants me to come to the party and it's on Saturday. Can you come and get me and bring me over for it, Kat?" Meggie pleaded. "Mum's going to be working."

Kat raised her eyebrows at Jess. "And does Miranda's mother know Miranda's invited you?"

Jess reached for her bag and held up an envelope. "Sorry. Forgot," she mouthed.

"Yes, of course, Kat. Miranda asked her first. Miranda and I have the same rules."

"I'm pleased about that," Kat said dryly. "What's your mother think about this?"

"Well." Meggie paused and sighed. "I kind of haven't told her yet. I thought you might sort of ring her and ask her if I can go."

"Meggs!"

"I'm sorry, Kat. But you know how Mum is. I was going to ask her last night when she got home from work, but she was really distracted. I think she might have had a fight with Tori." Meggie paused again. "She'll be home in half an hour."

"Meggie, we'll have to talk about all this next time I see you." Obviously Meggie was clued into playing her best cards with Kat and her mother so Kat decided she'd have to set some boundaries.

"Does that mean you aren't going to talk to Mum?" Meggie said disappointedly.

"No. I will talk to her. Jess is here now and she has the invitation."

"Oh. Great." Meggie's voice was full of smiles. "That's all right then. I'll go, Kat, so you can talk to Jess. She can tell you all about Caleb's party. She's really nice. I like her a lot. Don't you?"

"Yes. I do."

"Okay. 'Bye, Kat. Love you."

"Me too, you," Kat said and hung up.

"I meant to give you this when I arrived." Jess handed Kat the party invitation as Kat rejoined her.

The envelope had *Kat and Meggie* on the front in what was obviously Miranda's writing.

"Caleb wanted you and Meggie to come, but I'll understand if kids birthday parties aren't your thing," Jess said. "It will no doubt be mega-noisy and full on."

"No. That's okay. I teach eight-year-olds so I'm used to mega-noisy and full on. I can help out if you need me to."

"Heaven forbid." Jess laughed. "Unless you absolutely have to play Pin the Tail on the Donkey, you and I are going to enjoy ourselves. Mark and Lucas will be doing the hard work. I'm just the food person."

"Well, I'll help with that."

"You're hired."

"It was nice of Caleb to ask us," Kat said.

"Depending on what sort of party they're having we usually ask the kids to make a list of those they want to invite." Jess laughed. "And you and Meggie were on the list." She sobered. "Will there be a problem with Meggie being able to come?"

"I don't think so. She'll be staying with her grandparents this week so I'll just collect her from there and drop her back." Kat hoped it was going to be that simple. "I'll check with her mother when she gets home from work."

"It's just that Miranda's quite taken by Meggie." Jess shrugged. "Miranda can be a trifle, well, self-contained. That in itself isn't so bad usually, but Mark and I worry about her a little. She seems to have a lot of friends at school, but apart from Katie Farrelly, she doesn't have any close friends. Unfortunately Katie goes to a different school so they only see each other at cricket. Caleb, on the other hand, has three friends he's grown up with and they're best buddies."

Kat nodded. "Meggie's been just like Miranda. In my experience texting is part of daily life for kids. Now that Meggie's got her mobile phone I've been expecting her to be forever texting her school friends, especially with them being on school holidays, but she doesn't seem to at all. Yet she tells me she talks to Miranda every night."

"So she does." Jess laughed. "Mark teases them unmercifully, tells them they only have an allotted number of words per day, and they want to be careful they don't use up all their words in the middle of a sentence. I'm not sure that they don't believe him." Jess paused. "So you think you and Meggie will be able to come to the party?"

"I think so. We'd both love to come." Kat hoped there wouldn't be a problem with Shael. "Unless Meggie's grandparents have something planned."

"Meggie told Miranda her mother was an ophthalmologist. Miranda was very impressed."

"Yes. She is," Kat said carefully. "She has a private practice. She also works at the Royal Brisbane."

"Have you—? I suppose you've known each other a long time. You and Meggie's mother, I mean."

"About ten years. Meggie was only a couple of months old when I met Shael." Jess held Kat's gaze and Kat chattered on. "Shael's nieces attended the school where I was teaching, and Shael came along to one of the school concerts. We met then."

Kat could have told Jess at that time it had been a long painful year since she'd broken up with Ruth, and Kat hadn't been looking to start another relationship. She'd even told Em she'd sworn off women. Em's eyes had lit up, and she'd informed Kat she had a whole list of eligible guys waiting in the wings. But Kat had had to let Em down firmly but nicely on that score. She hadn't been interested, period.

Actually, Em had been at that same concert as one of her brother's children also attended the school, and Em's eyebrows had risen meaningfully when Shael, niece in tow, approached Kat.

"Natalie here tells me you're the famous Miss Oldfield," Shael had said.

"Famous? Oh dear," Kat replied, liking the tall, attractive woman with the deep, dark eyes. "Is that ominous?"

"Not at all." Shael laughed. "You're such a favorite of Natalie's the family kind of feels we know you. Nat's always talking about you. Miss Oldfield says this. Miss Oldfield says that. Don't you, Nat?"

Natalie blushed and rushed off to find her mother.

"Oops! I think I've embarrassed my niece. I didn't mean to." The woman held out her hand. "I'm Shael Smith, Natalie's aunt. Her least favorite aunt now, I'm thinking." The woman smiled into Kat's eyes.

Kat took the proffered hand, feeling a heady spark of feelings she thought Ruth had killed. "Kat Oldfield," she said. "And this is Em Martin. She also teaches here at St. Augustine's."

They'd stood chatting until it was time to return to the concert hall for the second half of the concert.

"Well!" exclaimed Em as Kat drove her home later that evening. "So that's how it's done."

"How what's done?" Kat flicked on the car's indicator and changed lanes.

Em blew a raspberry. "She's definitely interested. I don't even know what lesbians do and I could see that."

"See what? Who?" Kat made an attempt at nonchalance. "I don't know what you're on about, Em."

"Of course you don't. Not!" Em remarked sarcastically. "I'm talking about the dark and smoldering one. The lucky Natalie's aunt. Stop playing dumb."

"Em, come on!"

"So are you going to go out with her?" Em asked.

"Em you're being ridiculous."

"Well, I bet you anything you like she's a lesbian. I could tell."

"Don't tell me, Em. It was your gaydar going off that alerted you. Right?"

"Very droll, Kat. But I am right, aren't I? You could tell, too."

"It's not that easy, Em. Who knows for sure these days?"

Em murmured agreement. "True. But all I'm saying is, if she wasn't a lesbian she jolly well had no right to look at you the way she did."

Kat knew that was a fair comment, but she wasn't going

to tell Em that. Who knew where that sort of encouragement would take Em's conversation.

"So are you going to go out with her?" Em persisted.

"She didn't ask me." Kat shrugged.

"Well, get prepared, Miss Oldfield, because she will. That's another bet I'd lay good money on."

"Em, please. Leave it alone. I told you, I'm not looking to begin a new relationship. It's all too hard. And way too painful."

"I'll grant you that. It can be painful, but" —Em held up her finger— "think about the rest of it, if you know what I mean. She looks as though she'd be totally hot in bed."

"Em!" Kat cringed. "Now I'm embarrassed. And if I ever see her again, and I'm not saying I will, I won't be able to look her in the face."

"So look somewhere else. Wherever lesbians look. At her boobs or something. At least give her a clue you're a lesbian too. Next thing you know you'll be—"

"Em! Enough!"

"Oh, come on, Kat. You can't tell me lesbians don't have sex. I mean, if they don't then why are there so many lesbians?"

"It's not just about sex, Em," Kat began.

"Okay. Neither is hetero sex." Em rolled her eyes. "But the sex happens, doesn't it? We are reading the same book here, aren't we? Just different versions."

"Good grief! If I've said it once, I've said it a hundred times. Em, you're incorrigible." Kat turned into the driveway of Em's flat. "And I have to say I've never been happier to see the blue door of your apartment," she added with gusto.

Em laughed. "Just promise me one thing."

"Depends what it is."

"When she asks you, say yes."

"If she asks me, I promise I'll think about it."

Em planted a noisy kiss on Kat's cheek and climbed out of the car. "And I'll want a blow-by-blow account. About who did what, to whom."

"You wish," Kat ventured, her cheeks flaming.

Em was still laughing as she unlocked her door.

Three days later Shael had rung and asked Kat out. Kat

had said yes and the following few years, living with Shael and Meggie had totally revived Kat's love of life. In fact, Shael and Meggie had become the loves of Kat's life. And now it was over.

"So you've known Meggie since she was born?" Jess's voice dragged Kat back out of her reflections.

"Yes." She smiled. "She was all big eyes and dark hair standing up on her head. I often tell her she looked permanently startled. She was such a cutie. I couldn't love her more if she was my daughter. It's been a joy watching her grow up." Kat felt a lump close her throat and she swallowed. If Shael stopped her from seeing Meggie, Kat knew she wouldn't be able to bear it.

"I know what you mean," Jess said, her face softening in a quick smile that cut through Kat and circled her heart. "If there's one thing I have done in my life that I've never regretted, it's having the kids. Mark and I both agreed on that. Our marriage may have been a mistake, but all that was negated by having Miranda and Caleb." Jess paused, then seemed to come to a decision. "What happened to Meggie's father? She only mentioned him once, that morning at cricket."

Kat hesitated, trying to decide how to reply. What should she tell Jess? She really had no idea where the other woman stood on the controversial subjects of donor dads or lesbian mothers.

"I'm sorry, Kat. I didn't mean to pry," Jess put in quickly. "But I did, didn't I?" she added apologetically. "I just didn't want the kids to say anything to Meggie about her father that wasn't appropriate. I was worried he'd passed away or something."

"No. He's still alive as far as I know," Kat told her. "But Meggie's never met him. He was a friend of her mother's and as he didn't want to be part of Meggie's life they, Shael and Meggie's biological father, decided it would be best if he wasn't on the scene."

"Oh. I see. That's sad. For Meggie and for him. He's missing out on knowing a wonderful person."

Kat smiled. "Absolutely. You'll get no argument from me on that score."

"You've never thought about having children yourself?" Jess asked.

"I would have liked to have had children when I was younger but, well, the time was never right." Kat grimaced. "And now I'm getting a little long in the tooth as they say."

"Rubbish." Jess admonished. "You aren't that old."

"Thirty-four." Kat grimaced. "And twenty-four seemed like only yesterday."

"I know what you mean." Jess laughed her wonderful laugh. "And thirty-four is not old. Besides, lots of women are waiting to have children until their thirties these days." Jess's voice dropped slightly. "It's such a shame you don't have kids. You're so good with Meggie."

"Thanks. Having the opportunity to watch Meggie grow up has been fantastic."

The past raised its head inside Kat again. She'd wanted to have a child, and the subject had caused her first argument with Shael. Meggie had been about two years old. Kat had suggested she have a baby, that it would be good for Meggie to have a brother or sister. Shael had been adamant in her refusal to even contemplate the issue. She wanted no disruptions in her life at that stage. She was trying to set up her practice, and she was working long hours. It was all she could do to cope with one toddler, let alone a newborn.

Kat hadn't pushed the idea in the beginning because she knew Shael was working so hard. Shael left before Kat rose in the morning so Kat would organize Meggie to daycare, put in her day teaching, collect Meggie on her way home, feed and bathe her. More often than not Meggie had been asleep before Shael got home. And every time Kat mentioned another child Shael had always had a valid excuse. Maybe in a few years, she'd said on any number of occasions. And now it was too late.

"It's obvious Meggie cares for you," Jess was saying.

Kat laughed then. "Yes. Meggs and I are your typical mutual admiration society."

"Wasn't there an old song about that?"

"I think so. At least Em's parents used to sing it to each other, much to the embarrassment of their offspring. They had loads of old LPs that had belonged to Em's grandparents. Em's parents had and still have a wonderful marriage."

"Have you, well," Jess pushed a strand of fair hair behind her ear, "thought about marriage yourself?"

Kat hesitated again. This was her chance. But what if Jess was homophobic? What if she saw homosexuality as an abomination like Kat's parents and any number of other people? She'd never given Kat any indication that this might be so, but could Kat take the chance on losing this budding friendship she had with Jess? Yet, could she just be a friend to Jess when she wanted to be so much more?

"Uh! Oh! I'm prying again, aren't I?" Jess had misconstrued Kat's silence and Kat hurried to reassure her.

"No. It's okay. I was trying to think of an answer."

Jess raised her eyebrows. "And the answer is?"

"Um. No, I guess."

Jess chuckled. "Well, that's a relief. I was thinking you had a terrible broken engagement or divorce in the past, and it was still too painful to talk about."

"No. Not exactly. Well, I did have a broken relationship and it was painful, but I have moved on." Kat stopped, realizing she was thinking in the very final past tense. Her breakup with Shael had been extremely painful, but it was in the past. She really had moved on. Em would be ecstatic with Kat's progress, and Kat sensed an *I told you so* hovering on the horizon.

"I'm sorry, Kat," Jess said with sincerity and Kat nodded.

"But we weren't married," she finished and her gaze met, held, Jess's. And Kat knew it was time. "Actually, there is something I feel I should talk to you about. About me, I mean. I don't exactly talk about it to a lot of people," she paused.

"Well, feel free to talk to me," Jess said easily.

"I'm just concerned—" Kat stopped again and when Jess remained silent, Kat continued in a rush. "I prefer women," she said quickly. "I'm a lesbian."

The word echoed into the silence that stretched between them.

CHAPTER SIX

"I think I guessed that," Jess said softly.

"The big letter *L* in the middle of my forehead gave me away, hmmm?" Kat tried for humor and Jess laughed.

"No. Meggie mentioned you and her mother as a pair, and I sort of put two and two together. Not that it matters—" Jess broke off as Kat's phone rang.

Kat looked at the offending machine, trying to decide if she'd answer it or not. But it might be Meggie again. She pulled a face. "Sorry, Jess. Will you excuse me." She lifted the phone just before it went to messages. "Hello."

"Kat? It's Em's mum," said a familiar voice.

"Hi, Em's Mum! How are you?" Kat said brightly, picturing

Mrs. Martin in the kitchen at this time of day, cooking up a delicious meal for whichever family members were at home at that moment. She smiled as she heard the muffled sounds of children, the background noise synonymous with the Martins.

"I'm fine, love. And you?"

"Great." Kat glanced across at Jess as she stood up, pointed to her watch and the door, miming that it was late and she had to go. Kat was torn. "Excuse me a minute," she said to Mrs. Martin. She covered the mouthpiece. "It's Em's mother. I shouldn't be too long."

"It's okay, Kat. I should go anyway. Mark and Lucas and the kids will be home now. Thanks again for the toasted sandwich and for, well, being a great listener. So." She smiled. "We'll see you and Meggie at the party on Saturday?"

"Sure thing." Filled with uncertainty and regret, Kat watched her leave. She hadn't seemed to be upset by Kat's revelations, but perhaps she was just being polite. She uncovered the mouthpiece and apologized to Em's mother.

"I didn't mean to interrupt when you have guests."

"Just a friend. She was leaving anyway. What's up?" And suddenly it occurred to Kat that something may be wrong with Em. Now that she thought about it, she hadn't heard from Em for days. "Is Em all right?"

Em's mother gave a soft laugh. "She's fine. She's gone up to Townsville for the week with Joe. He had a job tender to do up there so at the last minute Em decided it was a good opportunity for them to get away so she went with him."

"Oh. That's great."

"Why I'm calling, Kat, is because your father rang me."

"Dad rang?" Kat was nonplussed.

"Mmm. He'll probably be ringing you anytime now. You see, he wanted your phone number and under the circumstances I felt I had to give it to him. I just hope I've done the right thing, that it was all right with you."

"Sure," Kat said carefully. "You said, under the circumstances. What did he want? Was there something wrong?"

"He said your mother hasn't been well. They're not sure what it is but she's having tests. He did sound worried, Kat."

"Oh."

"Kat, I know you and your parents are estranged but with your mother ill, maybe it would be a good time for you to make contact with them again. It's such a shame, and we just never know what's ahead of us."

"Right," Kat said reluctantly. What could be wrong with her mother? She'd hardly had a day sick as far as Kat knew. And if it was that serious then why hadn't Beth contacted her. "And Dad didn't say what was wrong with Mum?"

"No. Oh, Kat. If Em was here I'd send her over to your place."

"It's okay," Kat reassured her. "I'll ring Dad and talk to him."

"I'd come over myself, but I'm here on my own and I've got some of the grandchildren sleeping over tonight. But, Kat, I can't help but feel it must be something serious if your father wants to talk to you."

"I'll ring him," Kat assured her.

"And you let me know if I can do anything to help." Em's mother rang off.

Half an hour later Kat was still sitting staring at the phone. Her emotions kept wavering between guilt and justification. They hadn't spoken in years. Why should she change the situation.? She was happy with things the way they were. She didn't need any extra stress in her life. Yet she knew Em would tell her to ring her father immediately. Em wouldn't have hesitated because her relationship with her parents was so different from Kat's.

Angrily, Kat stood up and stalked the length of the living room and back. It was her life, her decisions, her choices. She was thirty-four years old, and it was time she took charge of her own life. No depending on others. Not Em. And not Shael. She was on her own.

She sat down again. So what to do? Her mother was ill. Surely her father wouldn't call if it wasn't serious. In fact, Kat couldn't imagine her father making a decision without her mother's direction. And then she felt ashamed of herself. No matter how she perceived her father he was just that. Her father. He'd raised her, gone to work, held a responsible job at the bank, come home and cared for her mother, who was at best a difficult person. She knew she had to make the call.

Still she hesitated. Should she ring Beth instead? Surely her father would have spoken to Beth. And surely Beth would have rung Kat if it was that serious. The whole situation, to quote a well-known sci-fi character, was illogical.

The bottom line was that her mother was ill, she reminded herself. She reached for the phone and dialed the number she hadn't known she remembered.

Her father's voice sounded the same as it had all her life. But older. She realized he must be in his mid-seventies now. And suddenly she wanted to call back the days of innocence when the child in her had accepted her life as her life. No regrets. No expectations.

"It's Kat," she said, her voice sounding thick.

"Katrin," her father said, and Kat was sure his voice broke.

Silence echoed over the line.

"Em's mother told me you wanted to talk to me, that Mum wasn't well."

"I was just going to try you again. I rang this morning and got an answering machine, but it was a different number to the one Mary Martin gave me today."

"I've moved house," Kat explained, wondering what Shael would make of the call if her father had left a message. "What's wrong with Mum?"

"She's in Hospital, the Royal Brisbane. I just came home to change and get a bite to eat. I was about to go back."

"What's... when did she go to Hospital?"

"Yesterday. They think it's her heart. They're doing tests."

"How serious is it?" Kat asked as her father coughed, obviously upset.

"I don't know. That's the trouble. Your mother tells me one thing and the doctors another. Your mother's not the best of patients."

"No. I suppose she isn't." Kat had no difficulty believing that.

"I just don't know what to think." Her father sounded desperate. "But your mother's, well, she's worried, that she won't make it. She looks so pale. I'm worried sick myself."

"You're off to the Hospital now?"

"Yes. For the meal time. I try to coax her to eat, but she isn't fussed on the hospital food. She won't even give it a try so I'm taking something with me in the hope she'll eat that."

"Have you rung Beth?"

"Yes. She's away south on business. But she's got a flight home tomorrow morning."

"Okay. Well, I'll come up to the Hospital. I'll meet you there."

Her father sounded relieved as he gave her ward and room numbers and directions once she got to the Hospital.

Kat was a mass of jumbled, jousting nerves as she walked along the colorless hospital corridor, her shoes making a peculiar squeak on the polished floor. Conflicting emotions fought for a hold inside her, coupled with an unwelcome surprise at the depth of her concern for her mother. Throughout Kat's life they'd never been on the same wavelength, but her mother was her mother and Kat loved her, even though there was never any indication that her love was reciprocated. Not the way Em's mother showed overwhelming love for her family.

As the thought skittered about in her head, Kat knew it wasn't totally fair of her to compare the two women. Their personalities, their entire beings, were poles apart in every respect. Physically, Em's mother was plump and cuddly, always smiling, while Kat's mother was a small, gaunt woman with sharp features. And Kat couldn't remember her mother laughing out loud. Yet all this wasn't her mother's fault. She couldn't change her basic persona anymore than Kat could.

Kat hesitated as she came to the hospital ward. She walked up to the nurse's station, gave the young nurse her mother's name and explained she was the patient's daughter.

"Oh, yes. Ann Oldfield. Room five. You've just missed your father. He won't be long though. He's just popped down to the canteen. Your mother fancied something sweet."

Kat felt another twinge of guilt. She knew her mother was

fond of chocolate. She should have stopped and bought some for her, but she'd been so wrapped up in her ambivalent concern for her mother she hadn't given such things a thought. But if her mother was allowed chocolate, surely— "How is she?" Kat managed to ask, but she could glean nothing from the nurse's face.

"As well as can be expected. Heavily medicated, I'm afraid." The nurse smiled encouragingly. "But go on in. I'm sure she'll be pleased to see you."

Somehow Kat seriously doubted that. But her father *had* made the effort to contact Kat after all.

"She may drift in and out of sleep," the nurse continued, "but she'll know you're there. Room five. Off to the left."

Kat headed down another hallway, hesitating in the doorway of Room five.

It was a single room. Her mother lay in a narrow bed, propped up on pillows and hooked up by wires and cables to various devices that rippled and blinked with data. Kat silently approached the bed, trying not to focus on the readouts on the machines.

Her mother looked impossibly smaller and older, her hands lying lifelessly on the neatly folded pale blue hospital bedspread. Her hair, neatly combed by a nurse or her father, was completely grey now, and her face was lined and careworn.

Kat's emotions went into confused overdrive again and inexplicable tears welled in her eyes. She swallowed painfully, gradually getting herself under control again. Her mother's eyes were closed, and she seemed to be sleeping so Kat decided she'd just stand and wait for her father to return. He shouldn't be long. She took a soft step closer, and her mother's eyelids fluttered open.

"Mum?" Kat said softly.

Her mother's head moved from side to side.

Kat bit her lip. Did that mean her mother didn't want her there? "Mum. It's Kat. Katrin," she added. She chanced a quick glance at the machines, but none of them seemed to be changing tone to an alarm.

"Katrin?" repeated a weak voice. "Your father rang then?"

"Yes. How are you?"

Her mother's lips trembled, and one hand fluttered on the bedspread. "I'm finished, Katrin."

"Don't say that, Mum," Kat implored gently.

"I know how I feel, and I know I'm finished."

"Dad says the doctors are doing lots of tests. I'm sure—"

"The doctors are all children, just out of school," her mother said imperiously, her voice stronger. "What do they know?" Her mother's eyes closed again, and Kat thought she'd drifted back to sleep. She sank down onto the chair close to the bed where her father had obviously been sitting.

"Katrin?"

Kat sat forward and found herself taking her mother's hand in hers.

Her mother looked down at their hands, and her fingers tightened around Kat's. "I told your father to ring you, to tell you I wanted to see you."

"Mum, you should rest."

Ann Oldfield shook her head slightly again, a frown on her face. "My time's come, and I suppose I've had a good life, easier than some, and there are things I need to tell you." She coughed and indicated she wanted water.

Kat poured some from the pitcher on a freestanding tray, lifted the tumbler and held the straw to her mother's lips. She drank sparingly, then her head rested back on the pillows.

"I need to tell you the truth."

"Mum, it's all right. We don't need to talk now. You aren't well enough. It will tire you out." Kat silently wished her father would hurry back or that the young nurse would come in to check on her mother.

"That's why I have to tell you now, Katrin. Don't you see?"

"It's all in the past, Mum. Let's leave it there. We both said things, well, I know I said things I regret."

"Yes. I have regrets too. And I need to tell you something you should know. I'm tired of secrets."

"Secrets?" Kat frowned, wondering if the medication was responsible for her mother's words and thoughts. "Look, Mum, Dad will be back soon, and you shouldn't be upsetting yourself."

"I blame myself," her mother said, "for your abhorrent behavior."

Kat stiffened. So there appeared to be no change in her mother's opinion. For a moment Kat had thought—

"Are you still living with that woman?" her mother asked. "That Dunleavy woman."

"No." So her mother hadn't heard about Ruth's death. And Kat had never told her parents about Shael and Meggie. The fiasco with Ruth had destroyed any need or desire to share information with her parents. "I'm on my own now."

"That's a blessing then."

"But I'm still a lesbian, Mum. That won't change," Kat said softly.

"It's such an awful sounding word." Ann Oldfield moved her head again. "But no matter. It's all my fault. I take the blame." She drew a rasping breath.

"Mum, it's no one's fault. It's just how and who I am. No one turned me into a lesbian. I just am."

"But I'm to blame." Her mother's hand fluttered to her mouth then fell back on the bed. "I'm so tired."

"You have to rest, Mum. We'll talk later."

"No. Please. Katrin, listen." Ann Oldfield closed her eyes for long moments as Kat sat bemused.

What could her mother tell her that was so important? Theirs was a run-of-the-mill family, a boring family some might say. And apart from Kat's lesbian relationship with the much older Ruth there was nothing out of the ordinary. Her father had worked in a bank. Kat swallowed. Had he done something illegal? No. Kat couldn't see her father in that role. As far as Kat knew, her mother still worked part time for the company she'd been with for forty years or so. Beth, her sister, was a businesswoman, successful and well-respected. Kat could think of nothing.

"I thought I was doing the right thing. I did it for the best. For Beth and for you." Her mother stopped to catch her breath again. "Your father agreed with me. We thought it would give you and Beth, but especially you, a better chance in life."

"I understand, Mum." Kat awkwardly patted her mother's

hand. "Why not have a rest now. I'm sure the doctors don't want you tiring yourself. And Dad will be back soon."

"I need to say this before he comes back. He didn't want— No matter. It has to be done before I go. You see, Beth was still at school. She had no real interest in the boy and neither of them were in any position to support themselves. We didn't want you to go to a stranger. John didn't think it was right. He said you were family. So we kept you." The last came out with a fit of coughing.

"Mum?" Kat sat looking at the woman in the hospital bed. "What are you trying to say? I don't understand?"

Her mother dabbed at her mouth with a tissue. "I didn't give birth to you, Katrin. Beth did. She got herself into trouble as we used to say when I was a girl. She had you and we kept you."

CHAPTER SEVEN

Kat could literally feel the blood drain from her face. If she hadn't been sitting down her legs would have given way beneath her. It was as though her mind and her body had parted company. She heard the words. She examined them. But they made no sense.

"Beth?" She barely realized she'd said her sister's name aloud. No. Not her sister. "No. I don't believe you." The words seemed to drift from somewhere far away. Slowly she pushed herself to her feet.

"I thought you needed to know," Ann Oldfield said.

"Why?" Kat got out. "Why would you think that?"

"It's the truth. I needed to tell you the truth."

Kat was still having trouble comprehending. Her whole life had been turned upside down. It had all been a lie. She had to get away from here. She shouldn't have come. She should have left everything as it was, with the space between them. If she had, all this would never have happened.

"I have to go," she said then and her mother's head moved from side to side again.

"Katrin. I meant it all for the best," she said brokenly, and Kat saw a tear overflow and run down the weathered cheek.

Kat's emotions spun out of control again. She was totally awash in a disorienting mixture of compassion, recrimination, disbelief and despair. "I have to believe that," she said, almost to herself. "I have to go now. I have to think. About this. About everything."

"Will you," Ann Oldfield swallowed, "come back?"

"No. Yes. I don't know. I have to think it through." Kat turned and walked out of the room, down the short corridor, past the now unattended nurse's station, along the passage towards the elevators. As she approached them the lift's doors pinged open and her father stepped out. No. Not her father. *Her grandfather.*

John Oldfield was still lean, his body straight, belying his seventy odd years, but his face was drawn and lined with worry. Kat could only stare at him as though she'd never seen him before.

"Katrin!" His worried face creased into a smile. "I'm sorry. I thought I'd be back before you got here. Your mother felt like ice cream." He held up the plastic bag in his hand. "She's never really fancied ice cream but no matter, long as she has something. Did you see your mother?"

Kat couldn't find her voice, and the smile on her father's face faded and his face paled.

"She hasn't— What's happened?" he asked in a choked voice.

"She's all right," Kat got out.

"Oh. Thank God! I thought—" He cleared his throat. "You're looking well. You've barely changed. Maybe your hair's a little shorter than it was."

Kat gulped a breath. "Mum told me," she said flatly and he frowned.

"Told you? What did she say? About what the doctors said?" He shook his head a little. "Look, love, I think we both, your mother and I, were panicking a little. The doctor came around just before I went downstairs. He's going to do an angiogram tomorrow just to be on the safe side. Your mother's been thinking heart attack or cancer. They've ruled out cancer, but your mother's not convinced. She's not herself. Look, there's a lounge just down there. Let's go in there. It's private."

Kat let her father take her arm and guide her through a glass-topped door into a small room with a group of comfortable easy chairs, low tables piled with magazines, an almost full bookshelf and a television set.

"Sit down, Kat. And we'll talk." He waited until Kat sank into a chair then sat down opposite her. "I thought originally that your mother'd had a stroke, but the doctors ruled that out too. They've had to keep her fairly heavily sedated because she gets so agitated. She keeps apologizing to me for, well, things I can't recall happening." He shook his head. "I think the doctors are now considering the possibility it could be psychological."

"Dad, stop." Kat held up her hand. "I didn't mean—I meant she told me the truth. About me. And Beth."

Impossibly, her father's face lost more color. "I don't know what you mean. She's not herself. You can't—"

"She told me I'm your granddaughter. Are you saying that's not true?" Kat asked him flatly.

"I—I don't know why—" John Oldfield ran a hand over his jawline, shook his head and swallowed. "Katrin. Your mother's not well."

"For heaven's sake, Dad. Just tell me if it's true or not."

Her father's gaze fell from hers. "She shouldn't have told you," he said at last, his voice thick with emotion. "I thought we'd discussed it. I thought we'd decided not to say anything. I can't understand why she had to tell you. It serves no purpose."

"She seems to think she's dying and needed to confess," Kat said and her father flinched. He stood up, paced the small carpet square.

"She's not dying. The doctor's told her. I've told her." He

rubbed his jaw again. "My God, what a mess. What am I going to tell Beth?"

"You might consider the truth."

He walked back, sank down in the chair again. "At the time I tried to talk your mother out of the idea of keeping it all a secret. But she was horrified Beth was pregnant out of wedlock. I didn't feel as strongly about it as your mother did. It was just that Beth was so young, just a child herself. She hadn't even finished high school. And she scarcely knew the boy."

"Has Beth talked to you about it? Since, I mean," Kat asked.

"No. Never."

Silence fell between them, Kat's mind racing at a hundred miles an hour as she tried to fit it all into place. But that was the problem. Nothing fit. It was as though her life was a jigsaw puzzle and none of the pieces fit. They were the pieces belonging to someone else's puzzle.

She stood up. "I have to go." She crossed to the door.

"Will you come back?" His words echoed his wife's.

Kat turned, shook her head. "I don't know. It's all too new. I have to think it through."

"I wish you would, Katrin."

"It's Kat," she said petulantly.

He nodded. "Kat. We'd like to see you. Your mother and I, well, we do love you both." When Kat made no comment he stood up slowly, picked up the shopping bag with the ice cream for his wife and followed Kat into the hall.

She walked over to the elevators and pushed the down button. When she turned back he was still standing there. He lifted his hand and then headed back down the hallway. And it seemed to Kat that he had aged in that short half-hour.

Kat got through the next couple of days by throwing herself into her house renovations. Assembling the modular drawers and hanging space in her walk-in wardrobe took all her concentration. Translating the complicated instructions kept her mother's revelations mostly at bay. Then there was Caleb's birthday party. She collected an excited Meggie and drove to the Andrews' house. Being with Jess assured any other thoughts were at least temporarily pushed to the back of her mind.

So when Jess dropped in the next day to return the towel Meggie had left behind after Caleb's party, Kat was inordinately pleased to see her. Kat knew she shouldn't be, but somehow Jess's appearance always lightened her mood. Her heightened awareness of Jess seemed to brighten, to clarify the world around her.

"Come and have a look at the walk-in robe," Kat said, trying to keep the excitement out of her voice.

Kat had walked into her bedroom before she realized the intimacy of the situation. Before, the room had been bare. Although she'd only put on the first coat of paint on the walls, the room now held her new queen-sized bed and a pair of bedside tables. She glanced at Jess.

Jess was looking around, her gaze pausing on Kat, and Kat saw the movements in her throat as she swallowed before glancing quickly away. Kat's nerve endings went immediately to full alert. She turned and crossed to the walk-in robe. She knew Jess followed her because she could all but feel her there, so close behind her.

"It's starting to look like your place now," Jess said evenly as Kat slowly turned in the close confines of the wardrobe.

"I took your advice about the modular units," she said hastily, her voice sounding forcedly bright. "The guy down at All-Systems was really helpful."

"Was it Jeff?"

Kat nodded.

"The best thing is he's practical."

"He was, too." Kat indicated the right wall of the robe. "I just have this section to finish. There's plenty of hanging space, and I got an extra set of drawers."

"Did you have any trouble putting it together?" Jess asked and Kat laughed softly.

"Well, a few questionable words floated out into the ether. But it was fairly straightforward. Eventually."

They stood in the ever shrinking wardrobe, and Kat felt her physical reaction to Jess's nearness escalate to dangerous proportions. The closet had seemed so spacious until Kat had to share it with Jess. Kat swallowed as her mouth went dry. Her body was so aware of Jess, and long dormant shivers of desire played around in the pit of her stomach.

Kat knew she had to difuse the situation, and she hoped Jess didn't feel the growing tension swirling about them. She had to get them out into the open where Kat could move away from the pull of Jess's attraction. But she didn't seem to have control of her muscles. They refused to take direction. So she stayed where she was, drinking in every nuance of Jess's movements, her body, the tilt of her head, the profile of her face, her forehead, her small upturned nose, her strong chin, the way her fair hair curled around her ear and the creamy curve of her neck that invited a long, slow, nibbling kiss. There was a small freckle on the narrow expanse of skin showing where the open collar of her shirt folded back.

Jess's hand reached out and ran lovingly along the white melamine of the chest of drawers. How Kat wished that small tapering hand was moving over her skin in just the same way. She looked up to meet Jess's inquiring gaze and blushed with embarrassment. What had Jess said? Kat coughed. "I'm sorry."

Jess smiled, her beautiful mouth curving upwards, unknowingly torturing Kat. "I just said you've done a great job putting all this together. Sometimes the modular units can be tricky."

"Okay, so it was a bit of a challenge at times," Kat admitted. "I kept telling myself I was quite capable of following a list of instructions, to just remain calm and logical. Eventually everything seemed to fall into place." Kat also ran her hand over the surface of the dividing partition. When she looked back Jess was regarding her, her expression unreadable. Kat met her gaze and couldn't look away. She was drowning in Jess's clear blue eyes.

An eon passed as they stood looking at each other, unable to break the heightened connection. The tension in the confined space grew until Kat thought she could feel her body being bombarded by the charged particles. She wanted to escape, but she remained transfixed.

Then Jess's small white teeth bit down on her lower lip and Kat's gaze slid to settle there. She could see the fine white line delineating their shape, and she wanted to trace that line with her tongue tip. She bit back a low moan.

Time was immeasurable. A second or an hour passed. Kat felt disoriented and shaky, her legs weak, and she let her backside rest against the chest of drawers to steady herself. Suddenly heat surged through Kat's body and her eyes widened in surprise. She looked down in disbelief to see that Jess's hand covered hers. Kat knew she had to be dreaming, a wonderful, sensational, mind-blowing dream. Her gaze rose to meet Jess's again.

Jess's eyes had darkened to inky blue and her lips quivered imperceptibly. Kat felt herself leaning forward—or perhaps it was Jess. Then their lips met.

Desire tumultuously rose to thunder inside Kat. She tasted, nuzzled Jess's mouth, drew back, touched, tasted again. Soft, she thought, so soft. So tantalizingly soft.

Kat's arm slid around Jess's waist, drawing her closer. She turned slightly, rested back against the chest of drawers, settling Jess against her body, molding her to her contours. Kat's hands cupped Jess's buttocks, drew her closer and Jess made a low throaty sound. Kat's tongue tip slipped between Jess's lips and their bodies strained together. Kat felt every nuance of Jess's movements, the thrust of her breasts, the way her pelvis moved, the so loud, so sensual sound of her gabardine-clad thighs as they rasped against Kat's.

Somehow Kat had pulled Jess's shirt from the belted waist of her tailored shorts. She shakily unbuttoned Jess's shirt and moaned softly as she slid her hands over the smooth bare skin of Jess's midriff. She moved her hands slowly upwards to cup her lace-clad breasts.

Jess made an incitingly low and so-inviting sound. Kat felt her breath on the curve of her neck as Jess's body seemed to collapse against Kat's. Jess moaned again and the sybaritic sound sent clamors of wild desire from the pit of Kat's stomach to her centre.

She moved her hips against Jess's, her fingertips finding, teasing Jess's nipples. Jess's head went back, exposing the curve of her throat, and Kat slid her mouth over the smooth skin, nuzzling the soft spot where her pulse beat an erratic tattoo. And it was so much more headily intoxicating than she could have imagined.

Jess's hands clutched at Kat's head as she whispered Kat's name in a low husky tone that sent Kat's lips searing downwards to cover one hardened nipple with her mouth.

"Oh, Kat," Jess repeated as she strained against Kat. Her hands were unsteady as she fumbled for the bottom of Kat's T-shirt, lifting it up. She groaned again when she discovered Kat wasn't wearing a bra. Jess drew back, gazing down at Kat's breasts, her lashes dark curves against her cheek. "Kat," she breathed again as her fingers circled, teased Kat's nipples. Then she slowly lowered her head and put her lips to one rosy peak and then the other, sucking, flicking Kat's nipples with her tongue tip, exquisitely torturing.

Kat knew she was soaring, hovering on the brink of completely losing control. Her shaky knees demanded she sit, and the edge of the chest of drawers bit into her buttocks. She drew back, cupped Jess's beautiful face in her hands. Jess's fingertips replaced her lips, continuing to tease Kat's breasts, and Kat's back arched as her nipples thrust upwards, clamoring for the renewed feel of Jess's mouth.

"Jess! I have to—I need to—" She moved Jess through the closet door into the bedroom, and they both looked at the large, inviting bed.

Kat's body was way ahead of her, screaming for the comfort of the bed, for the feel of Jess's naked body against her. She kissed Jess again, gently, softly, a tentative appeal, and Jess kissed her back. Their kiss deepened and desire enveloped them again. Kat's kiss was a question and Jess's kiss the answer Kat needed. They began to move towards the bed.

"Yoo-hoo!" came a voice from the front of the house.

Kat and Jess stilled, bodies pressed together, lips on lips.

"Kat? Jess? Are you there?"

They sprang apart, and Kat looked down at Jess. Her shirt

was unbuttoned and gaping out of the waistband of her shorts, baring her lace-covered breasts. Kat's T-shirt was bunched up under her arms, her breasts bare and still aroused. Jess's hands rested on Kat's hips as her face suffused with color.

"Kat!" she breathed, her eyes seeking an escape. "It's Grace." She hurriedly tucked her shirt back into her shorts, but her hands were shaking so much Kat had to help her with the buttons. Jess looked at Kat's still bare breasts and her expression mirrored Kat's own still-surging desire.

Hurriedly Kat pulled down her shirt and settled it over her hips before running her fingers through her tousled hair. Her breasts were tingling and proud, and she pulled at the front of her shirt so it didn't cling so closely. She swallowed. "It's okay," she said softly, running a fingertip down Jess's flushed cheek before she took a deep breath and strode to the bedroom doorway.

Grace Worrall stood at the open front door, a tea towel covered plate in her hand.

"Oh. Grace. How are you?" Kat's voice was almost steady. "Come on in."

Grace stepped inside and Kat shot a quick look behind her. Jess was still straightening her clothes and didn't meet Kat's gaze.

With her legs still shaking, Kat walked into the living room, feeling Jess moving behind her.

"Hello, Grace," Jess said, her voice raspy, and she coughed. She moved into the kitchen and made a show of examining the fit of the cupboard doors.

"I was just showing Jess the new units I've put in the wardrobe," Kat said quickly. She felt herself grow hot again as her mind flashed up replays of Jess in the wardrobe, the feel of her, the throaty sounds, the thrill of her touch.

"I'll have to have a look myself before I go," Grace said and turned to Jess. "Kat's doing wonders with the house, isn't she?"

"Yes, she is," Jess agreed, sliding some drawers in and out, diligently checking their movement.

"With your help of course," Grace added. "I've just made some fresh pikelets and I thought it should be time for you to break for afternoon tea."

"Oh," Kat glanced at her wristwatch. "So it is. I didn't realize how late it was. I'll put on the kettle." Kat joined Jess in the kitchen, put water in the jug and set it to boil. Jess moved into the living room with Grace. Kat took a steadying breath as she set out the mugs. "Tea or coffee?" she asked, turning back to the other two.

"Tea, thanks, dear," said Grace.

"Oh, I—" Jess looked at her own watch. "I'll have to skip the tea unfortunately. I still have a couple of calls to make I'm afraid." She shrugged ruefully and managed to smile.

"Well, here. Take a couple of pikelets with you to eat on the way." Grace uncovered the plate, removed the plastic lid and held it out to Jess. "Strawberry or apricot jam?"

"Oh, thanks, Grace." Jess took a pikelet with jam and a dollop of cream and bit into the mini pancake.

Kat watched Jess's lips settle around the pikelet and her knees almost gave way beneath her again as the desire that had barely ebbed rose inside her again.

"Delicious," Jess said as she moved towards the door. "Thanks again, Grace. You've done a great job in there, Kat." Jess coughed and more color rose in her cheeks. "I'll see you both. Enjoy your tea." And she was gone.

Kat couldn't have said what she did with the rest of the afternoon. Oblivious, Grace stayed for a cup of tea, and Kat knew she must have talked to her visitor but she'd have been hard-pressed to recall what they talked about.

And later, alone, she wandered about the house wanting to phone Jess, preparing any number of scenarios in her mind. But she didn't do it. She couldn't decide what she'd say to her.

At the birthday party the day before, sitting beside the pool with a bikini-clad Jess, Kat had ached for her. And after those moments alone with Jess she ached for her so much more. Yesterday she'd thought she'd hidden her secret longings behind the protective façade of her sunglasses.

All afternoon at Caleb's birthday party she'd been totally aware of every facet of Jess's body, tuned to her every move, her body achingly aware each time Jess touched her arm or simply smiled at her. Kat knew she'd been in a bad way, and she'd given herself stern lectures as she drove home after dropping Meggie back at her grandparents' house.

"Isn't Jess the greatest?" had been Meggie's parting remark.

If Meggie only knew.

Now, after those exquisite moments in Kat's walk-in wardrobe, all Kat's hungry yearning almost engulfed her. She knew she'd never felt quite this way before. Not even with Ruth.

Yesterday she'd known how she felt about Jess, how attracted she was to her. When Jess had touched Kat's hand Kat's senses had gone crazy, taking her breath away. She'd felt herself burn with wanting. And yet it had been so innocent.

They'd been reclining beside each other on loungers by the pool, relatively alone. Mark and Lucas were supervising an energetic game of cricket on the lawn nearby. The children's excited voices, Mark's encouragement of the bowlers, the barking of an ecstatic dog filled the air.

"Aren't you glad you came?" Jess had asked with a grin. "Not exactly quiet and serene, is it?"

Kat laughed. "I can hardly hear them." What if she told Jess everything—the sunshine on the water, the neatly trimmed lawns, the voices of the children faded into insignificance when Kat sat watching Jess stretched out so close and yet so far away from her. Jess's bikini was quite modest for the fashion of the day, but Kat knew she could drown in the smooth expanse of Jess's bare skin. Her wonderful breasts with their enticing cleavage, her bare midriff, her long, tanned legs. "Besides," she added quickly, "the sounds of happy children having fun is so much better than the sounds of unhappy, disinterested and bored kids."

"True." Jess raised her sunglasses and looked across at Kat. "I meant to tell you I like your board shorts. Shades of purple. My favorite color."

"Thanks." Kat was wearing beach shorts over her swimsuit. "My swimmers are so old I've been expecting them to split if I move suddenly, so, in case of accident they'll at least cover my embarrassment."

Jess laughed softly and let her sunglasses slide back on her nose, disguising her expression. "I've enjoyed this afternoon and your company," she said softly, the husky tone of her voice sending shivers of delight through Kat.

"Me, too. You've got a lovely place here."

"Thanks. We've plans approved for turning the loft over the garage into a self-contained apartment, and I'd thought of moving in there. However, it's working well for the kids with all of us in the main house. Unconventional I know, but it works for us, so we've sort of shelved the plans for a while."

A cricket ball landed between their chairs, and they both reached down for it at the same time. Kat had hold of the ball and Jess's hand folded around Kat's. They sat like that for long moments, watching each other behind the anonymity of their sunglasses. Then Jess slowly released Kat's hand, and Kat sat up to throw the ball back to Lucas.

Kat was hot, burning at Jess's touch, and it was some time before either of them spoke and before Kat's heartbeats slowed to anywhere near normal.

Was it any wonder the next day Kat had been so aroused in the confined space of the wardrobe with Jess so close. And she was under no illusions about what would have happened if Grace hadn't appeared.

When night fell Kat put off going to bed because she knew she wouldn't sleep. She was too tense, too totally aware. The feel of Jess—her lips, the thrust of her hips—was too real now, not simply a wishful fantasy anymore.

Eventually she drifted off to sleep but woke unrefreshed. By lunchtime, when she'd spent hours starting one project and then going on to another, not finishing any of them, she'd even resorted to phoning Em. When she got Em's answering machine she belatedly remembered Em was away, and she didn't know if she was disappointed or relieved that she couldn't unburden herself to her friend.

In the afternoon she picked up the telephone any number of times to ring Jess, but each time she hung up before her call went through, wanting and yet not wanting to hear Jess's voice, to talk about what had happened.

Later that afternoon Kat made herself return to the bedroom. If she didn't take control of this she'd be standing around simply seeing Jess everywhere. And the bedroom needed its final coat of paint. She covered everything with drop-sheets and got to work.

The paint roller sloshed across the paneling, gradually covering the bedroom wall. Usually Kat found the sound and the steady repetitive movements therapeutically restful, but today her thoughts were a jumble of memories, old and new. There was Jess of course. Here. Right here in this room. So captivating and alluring. And incredibly sexy. Jess kissing her the way Kat had wanted her to since the moment they'd met. And mixed in with it all was that mind-numbing evening at the hospital. It seemed to Kat that nothing she did would ever be restful again. Both scenes did looping reruns in her mind.

Reluctantly she forced herself to stop thinking about Jess. And when she succeeded in getting that to fade into the background, those other memories from her past flashed up in irregular starbursts of recall. People. Conversations. Long forgotten episodes from what she'd thought was her boring, eventless childhood. Her mother's revelations had turned that upside down.

And none of it now seemed real. They felt like someone else's memories, as though it was all part of someone else's life, a someone else whose life Kat had always seen as a pale replica of everyone else's life. Like Em's, for instance.

But dull or not, it had been Kat's life. Now it was all a huge lie, a sham. Kat felt as though the little she'd had went crumbling into dust and was swept away by the wild winds of truth.

Her mother, the woman she'd accepted as her mother, had never been demonstrative. There were no hugs, no cuddles. Not like Em's family.

Until Kat met Em when they started school together she hadn't known family life could be so different. The Martins were touchy-feely to the extreme and after the initial shock when they'd wrapped her into their midst, she'd become intoxicated with the joy of it all. The fun. The laughter. The love. At every opportunity she'd escaped to the wonderful Martin home.

Em's mother cooked, and the house was always filled with the divine scents of cookies or stews. The Martin children clattered noisily about the house like excited puppies. Em's mother had accepted Kat into the family like another daughter. When Kat went home with Em after school, Mrs. Martin welcomed Em home with a hug. And then she did the same with Kat.

Kat still remembered the first time Em's mother hugged her. Mrs. Martin was a short woman, slightly overweight—pleasantly plump, as she described herself happily. She'd pulled Kat into her ample bosom, holding her close, and she'd smelled of freshly baked cookies and the subtle hint of lavender. Kat had never felt such an overwhelming sense of safety. Then the flour on Mrs. Martin's apron had made her sneeze, causing much laughter and a bustling search for tissues. And when Kat left for home there was another hug. Kat knew she'd stayed alert so she was always nearby when Em's mother started hugging.

All this only served to make her own family life seem colder and, in the beginning, she'd been loath to invite Em to her own home. It was a small price to pay for the wonderful experience of Em's family.

Of course, Em had eventually put Kat on the spot by demanding they go to Kat's house to play. Nothing Kat could say would deter Em, and Kat had been sick with worry that her friend would find Kat's home so awful she wouldn't invite Kat back to hers.

Em had stood for a moment in the silent, dull house and then she'd asked Kat to show her her room. Kat had been mortified. Her room was a barren planet compared to the bright bedroom Em shared with her younger sisters. Kat had tried to explain that her parents might repaint the walls soon and that she was going to ask for the same color as Em's bedroom. Em had smiled as though she was secretly pleased, but she'd assured Kat her bedroom was fine, that she just loved the quiet. She'd rolled her eyes expressively and told Kat that the Martins were just so loud, loud, loud.

Kat quickly told Em she loved the noise of the Martin house, only to be told by Em that if Kat spent every day with the Martins she'd soon be cured of that but she hadn't been convinced. If Em had asked her there and then, Kat would have packed her bag and left with no regrets.

Although Kat knew she had it all in a better perspective now, she still felt a glowing warmth when she was with the Martin family. She'd always felt a slight sense of guilt that being with Em's family had always felt more like home than her own had.

Kat frowned. There'd be no more feelings of guilt. Now she knew that the small measure of "home and family" she'd got growing up, well, even that had been fiction. A small voice of reason struggled to the surface, suggesting her mother's revelations had at least answered a lot of Kat's unanswered questions. Like why her mother had been so distant, so unmotherly.

Kat made a soft indignant exclamation as she added more paint to her roller. She wasn't a stranger's child. She was Ann Oldfield's granddaughter, her own flesh and blood. Surely that would have counted for something, Kat reasoned. Yet how often had she heard her mother say that motherhood had ruined her career, that she could have been on the top of the corporate ladder instead of stagnating as a lowly office manager. Looking back Kat could see that dissatisfaction had always colored her mother's life. Still, for all Kat knew it had been there before Kat was born, firmly entrenched in Ann Oldfield's psyche.

Kat moved her focus to her father. He'd always been in the background, hidden behind a book or newspaper, silent and colorless and unsmiling. Her mother had talked at him, expressing her dissatisfaction, and if he'd ever retaliated Kat had never heard him. Perhaps he'd tried in the beginning before Kat was old enough to understand but Kat somehow couldn't see it. Her father had simply been the dull, shadowy figure who went to work and came home.

And Beth. She tried to find a memory of her sister in the family equation and couldn't. Her visits were rare and her interaction with Kat had been nonexistent. At least now Kat knew why.

What they did on the weekends Kat had no recollection. They rarely went out as a family. In fact, she couldn't recall one time, apart from a confusing and solemn drive to attend the funeral of her only grandmother. *Great-grandmother,* she reminded herself.

Em's father, on the other hand, always seemed to be there, playing cricket or football with his family in the large backyard.

He helped with homework, mended broken toys, and he put his arms around Em's mother. Often he'd kiss her, on her lips, right there in front of the family and Kat. The kids teased them, and one of Em's brothers would whistle until Em's mother shoved her husband away and told him to go mow the lawn or make himself useful getting in the washing. He'd go off laughing and Em's mother's eyes would follow him, a happy smile on her face. It had given a young Kat a funny feeling somewhere in her chest, a yearning for that in her own life. But she'd never seen her father so much as touch her mother.

With one last pass of the roller to finish the side wall, Kat straightened and flexed her stiff back muscles. She glanced at her wristwatch and told herself it was more than time for a break.

She finished cleaning her painting tools and went into the kitchen to set the kettle boiling. As she reached for her tea mug she heard a knock on the door. Jess. Her heartbeats did their Jess thing, and she walked around the breakfast bar to see a figure standing on the top step, silhouetted in the open doorway. Far too tall for Jess. Her heart sank ruefully. And far too thin for Em. Kat paused then took a couple of stiff steps before stopping in the middle of the living room as recognition dawned.

"May I come in?" asked a familiar yet strange voice from her past.

Kat swallowed, suppressing an urge to turn and run. She gave a small nod and turned to move closer to the breakfast bar, feeling the other woman move into the house behind her.

Taking a deep breath she turned to face Beth. She'd known on some level that this moment would come, but it was too soon for Kat. She made herself meet the other woman's gaze.

Their eyes were the same color, Kat recognized, and they had the same shaped face. Kat had always known that, she reminded herself. Why did this particular fact come into her mind now. They were the same flesh and blood, sisters, after all. No, she admonished herself. Not sisters anymore. They were much more than that.

Unconsciously Kat registered that a rapid pulse beat at the base of Beth's neck and she watched her swallow quickly too. Beth, it appeared, was as nervous as Kat. Then Beth looked away, her gaze taking in the partly renovated house. "Impressive," she remarked. "Em told me you were renovating a house."

Kat raised her eyebrows. "Em told you?" Kat didn't recall Em mentioning she'd seen Beth, let alone spoken to her.

"I saw her in the city the week before last I think it was." Beth explained and swallowed again. "It's a big job on your own."

"Yes. But I'm not exactly doing it alone. I have a great company doing a lot of it."

"Oh."

Silence fell between them, stretching uncomfortably as the tension rose. The kettle switched itself off with a click that seemed to reverberate around them.

Beth glanced past Kat towards the kitchen. "Perhaps we could... Can we have coffee?"

"Sure." Kat agreed reluctantly before escaping around the breakfast bar.

Beth slowly followed Kat but kept the length of the breakfast bar between them. "White, thanks. With one sugar," she said before Kat thought to ask.

Kat busied herself with the preparations, feeling Beth's eyes on her. She flashed a quick glance at the other woman and then examined the image.

Beth didn't look all that different to Kat. It must be at least a year, maybe eighteen months since they'd seen each other, and it didn't seem to Kat that Beth had aged at all in that time. And she must be, what, fifty years old. She was sixteen years older than Kat so she must be fifty.

Sixteen years older. The enormity of it all suddenly hit Kat. The woman before her had been pregnant and had a child at sixteen. Kat thought back to when she herself was sixteen and couldn't imagine how she would have felt in the same situation, to know she was having a child, to have to tell her parents.

Reaching for the coffee jar, Kat glanced at Beth again. She surreptitiously studied the woman she had always known as her much older sister. No one would even suspect what had occurred in the past.

Beth was tall, taller than Kat, slim and very well groomed, every inch the successful businesswoman Kat knew she was. Her hair was the same dark brown as Kat's, worn long and pulled back, not severely but tidily, into a loose chignon at the back of her head. Her makeup was flawless.

She wore a dark grey suit—jacket and skirt—with a pale dove grey shirt that coordinated beautifully. Small, bright studs glistened in her ears, and she had a matching pin on the lapel of her jacket. Beth wasn't a stereotypically beautiful woman, but she was certainly arresting.

Fourteen years ago Kat knew Beth had bought the small company she'd been with all her working life. When the owners decided to retire Beth had taken over. The company had something to do with job training and was highly successful and well-respected. All Kat's knowledge had come via Em and Em's mother. And even if Kat hadn't been estranged from her parents they would never have spoken about Beth's accomplishments—or Kat's for that matter. It wasn't their way.

A couple of years ago Em's younger sister began a job with Beth's company and, according to Em, had high praise for Beth. She was firm but fair. So, if it hadn't been for Em Kat would have known next to nothing about Beth's working life. And Em had probably seen more of Beth in the past few years than Kat had. Kat felt a momentary pang of guilt. She made herself force it away. She had no need to feel guilty, Beth hadn't sought Kat out either.

Kat frowned slightly as she poured hot water over the coffee grounds. Beth hadn't really figured in many, if any, of Kat's childhood memories. She had left home before Kat started school and she rarely came home. Kat chastised herself for not picking up on the signs. But why would she? She'd been a child. How would she have known? Kat knew she'd wanted to leave home as soon as she could do so. Why would it have been any different for Beth? And there had to have been the added incentive of knowing Kat was her child. If Beth had cared—

Kat added milk and sugar to Beth's coffee, surreptitiously watching her walk over to the window to look out at the now opened-out veranda. Kat set the mugs on the coffee table and returned with a plate of cookies. She indicated the best chair for Beth and as she rejoined her, Kat handed her a coffee.

"Thanks." Beth settled into the well-worn chair.

"I'm sorry the furniture's a bit basic, but I'm sort of making do."

Beth gave a faint smile. "Em told me you were all but camping out."

"Em seems to have had a lot to say," Kat said dryly.

"You know Em. She'd talk underwater."

They both sipped their coffee.

"I always liked her," Beth said and Kat raised her eyebrows. "Em." Beth clarified. "You always seemed to have fun with her."

"I did," Kat remarked with sincerity. "It saved my sanity on many occasions."

Beth's gaze fell to her coffee mug. "I suppose it did." She sighed. "It surely wasn't much fun at home."

"No. It wasn't."

Beth carefully set her coffee mug on the table before looking across at Kat. "I suppose we should talk. About that. And other things." She began to fiddle with her suit jacket, her fingers smoothing the lapels. "Dad told me Mum had, well..." She swallowed.

"Set the family skeletons jangling in the attic," finished Kat flatly.

"That's very poetic," Beth said with a crooked smile. Then she sobered. "She shouldn't have told you. There was no need, nothing to be gained by it. Not after all these years."

Only the truth. Kat's emotions swung like a pendulum as she tried to read the expressions that flitted across Beth's face. Was she embarrassed that she'd had an illegitimate child? That that child had turned out to be Kat? Kat the ungrateful, the rebellious, the perverted—all the other words her mother had used in the past flashed into her mind with their usual negativity, leaving poisonous debris behind them to niggle away at Kat.

"Perhaps she just wanted to clear her conscience," Kat put in, sounding heaps more gracious than she felt.

"I don't believe Mum had a conscience," Beth said softly. "She was a bitter, difficult woman before and when I...well, afterwards, it just made her worse."

"Would you ever have told me?" Kat asked and Beth looked quickly at her and away just as quickly.

"No. Yes. I don't know." She shook her head slightly. "Probably not. I don't think I ever wanted you to know."

"Why not?"

"Because I don't see that it serves any purpose." She made a fluttering gesture with her hand. "But that's by the by now. Mum *has* told you, and I think we should discuss it."

"You do?" Kat got the words out with difficulty.

"Yes. The longer we leave it the, well, more uncomfortable it will be?"

Uncomfortable. Well, it was certainly that, Kat reflected wryly to herself. She should just tell Beth to put it out of her mind, pretend her mother had continued to keep their secret. That would be the most comfortable situation for the emotionless Oldfields.

"I thought you might have some questions." Beth shifted in her chair, smoothed her suit skirt over her knees. "Or something," she finished.

Kat bit off a soft laugh. "You mean apart from why wasn't I told?" Kat watched Beth's gaze fall again. Her fingers ran along the seam of her skirt, and Kat noticed Beth's hands were shaking slightly. It was Kat's turn to sigh.

"Look, Beth, I'm sorry. I'm just finding it difficult to get around the fact that my shadowy older sister actually gave birth to me."

Beth's lips tightened, and a fleeting expression Kat couldn't quite fathom passed over her face. *Tell me on some level you cared,* Kat wanted to say. But part of her knew she may not be ready for that particular truth on top of the other raw truth. She was far too vulnerable.

"Why not just tell me it isn't true," Kat suggested. "Tell me Mum was probably drugged, that she didn't know what she was saying."

"No, I can't say that, Kat. I wish I could, but I'm afraid it is true," Beth said without intonation.

"Then tell me what happened," Kat probed, amazed that she suddenly wanted to know. At least she was sure that Beth would keep to the basics and wouldn't get into the emotional. That was the Oldfield way.

Beth took another sip of her coffee, replaced the mug on the coffee table. "Just the usual story. It happens everywhere all the time. I got pregnant. Mum decided I was too young and that she should raise you."

Kat gazed incredulously at her sister. No, her birth mother. "That's it?"

"Pretty much."

Kat expelled a loud breath. "I can't believe that's all you want to say, to tell me." So much for unemotional, she chastised herself, while the conflicting part screamed at her not to push the issue in case Beth told her something she'd find too painful to hear.

"That's the trouble, Kat. I don't know what to say to you. I never have known."

"Maybe you could start by telling me who my father was."

Beth hesitated again.

"Mum said you didn't know him very well."

A frown gathered on Beth's brow. "That's probably true on one level. We did spend a good deal of time together though, considering Mum's restrictions," she said and shook her head again. "But you can't really blame Mum for saying that because it's what I told her."

Kat made no comment.

"As you know, Mum was strict." She grimaced. "Unfairly so, I thought back then. She barely let me out of her sight. I tried to tell her I just wanted to have some fun, spend time with my friends. Nothing I said made any difference. Mum being Mum, she stood firm. I even appealed to Dad. As usual he deferred to Mum."

Kat wasn't surprised.

"Maybe I should have done what you did. Made friends with a good Catholic family." She gave a bitter laugh. "You know, I was really put out when I saw Mum letting you spend time with Em. She certainly didn't give me that latitude."

"I think she was just pleased I wasn't under her feet," Kat said. "But I didn't care. I didn't want to be under her feet anyway."

Beth held Kat's gaze again but made no comment for long

moments. "You know she—Mum—was engaged to someone else before she married Dad."

Kat was more than surprised.

"Apparently he broke it off before the wedding. I overheard Mum and Dad arguing once. I think Dad paid for the shortcomings of her ex-fiance."

Kat gave this some thought. "He could have said something. He didn't have to let her belittle him all the time."

"I know. It wasn't as bad when I was a child. I think Dad, well, really cares for her."

Kat gave an exclamation of disbelief and then remembered the drawn and fearful look on her father's face when she arrived at the hospital. She drew her attention back to Beth. "So how did you manage to get out to meet this unknown donor?"

Beth flinched a little and Kat felt bad again. "I'm sorry. I just…I'm not sure I can call him my father, that's all."

"I started sneaking out at night. I climbed down that tree outside my bedroom window. And after school when Mum and Dad were at work we, well, had the house."

"In your room?" Kat was incredulous. "But Mum sometimes came home from work early. Didn't you think about that?"

"No, not at the time. I didn't and she didn't. And then, well, I was pregnant." Beth shrugged. "Mum and Dad took Long Service Leave from work, and we went on an extended holiday."

"And then there were four," Kat said dryly. "Didn't anyone suspect?"

"Not that I know of."

"Did you love him?" Kat asked flatly.

Beth moved in her seat. "I was fifteen."

Kat held Beth's gaze.

"You know what it was like at home, Kat. Any bit of attention was love." She made a negating movement with her head. "Look, I'm not completely blaming Mum and Dad. I knew what I was doing. Well, as much as any fifteen-year-old knows what they're doing. I just didn't plan on getting pregnant. He had condoms, but neither of us had done it before so," she shrugged again, "it just happened."

"You didn't answer my question."

Beth raised her eyebrows, and part of Kat recognized the similarities between them. She saw herself in Beth's expression.

"I suppose I did love him," Beth said carefully.

"You also didn't tell me who he was. And did he know about me?"

"Kat, I see no need to go into all this—"

"But you're not looking at it from my place in the situation, are you?"

The silence stretched between them for long moments, until finally, Beth sighed. "I suppose I'm not. And I have to admit I'm finding it difficult to do that. You don't know how much I wish—" Beth paused, swallowed, then drew herself together. "All right. His name was John Pattison. He was sixteen years old and the cousin of a friend. He was here for a couple of months visiting from Adelaide. He'd gone before I realized I was pregnant. I never told him."

"Do you know where he is now?"

A myriad of emotions passed fleetingly over Beth's face before she shook her head. "No. Why would I? And I see nothing can be gained by stirring all this up."

"You don't feel he has a right to know about me?"

"No. Think about it, Kat!" Beth appealed. "We were both far too young. He's probably married, has a family. What's to be gained by throwing his life upside down."

"He might just want to know," Kat said softly.

"And what if he doesn't? Do you want to put yourself through that?" Beth asked.

Kat's emotions went into overload and her stomach churned. Perhaps Beth was right. She needed more rejections like she needed a hole in the head. She made herself change tack.

"Did you ever consider having an abortion?" she asked Beth instead.

"Not consciously. I didn't even realize I was pregnant for months. I must have been in some sort of denial. I kept judiciously ignoring the obvious signs. I was nauseous, and I put on a little weight."

"Mum didn't suspect?"

"No. I'd caught a cold or flu as well and it wouldn't clear

up so Mum made an appointment with the doctor. She was to take me herself then something came up at work so she decided I could go on my own. It wasn't our family doctor but he was pretty shrewd. He asked me if I was pregnant and it went from there. He was the one who brought up the subject of abortion, and then only to tell me I was too far along to have one."

"So you were stuck with me?" Kat put in wryly.

"I suppose I was. But, Kat, in my defense I don't think I would have wanted to terminate my pregnancy, even if Mum had wanted me to."

At this, they both went quiet, lost for long moments in their own thoughts.

"Looking back," Beth said at last, "I went into emotional shutdown. Mum stepped in and made the decisions. It was easier to let her."

"Do you have any regrets about that?" Kat asked carefully.

"Yes and no. I know I wasn't in any position emotionally to make any choices but—" She shifted in her seat again. "I don't want to lie to you, Kat. I think we both need for me to be honest. Even if Mum hadn't made the decision she did I probably would have put you up for adoption. I remember the doctor mentioning adoption to me as an option, but then Mum took control and that was that.

"You see, I'm not a very maternal person. I never was. When I was a child I didn't have any interest in dolls or dreamed about having children, a husband and family like my friends did. I couldn't see myself raising a child. Not then and not now. I made the decision not to have any, well, any more children."

"But you married Phil," Kat put in.

"Yes. Being married suits us both. And having children was never an issue with Phil. Apart from the fact that I was thirty-nine and far too old to be having children when we married, Phil has two sons from his first marriage."

"Phil was married before?" Kat was surprised. Beth had kept that to herself as well. "Did Mum and Dad know?"

Beth shook her head. "I didn't see any need to tell them. Phil had been divorced for ten years before we married. His ex-wife remarried, and he has little contact with his sons." She gave a slight shrug. "I suppose you could say Phil and I are birds of a feather."

"So what you're trying to say is the status quo is fine by you." Kat tried to keep the bitterness out of her voice. "You want everything to go on as though the family secret was still locked in the proverbial closet."

"Well, yes. And no." Beth bit her lip. "All I'm saying is I would find shifting gears from your sister to your mother pretty well impossible. I don't want to make any radical changes. I don't think I'm capable of doing that."

"And you think it would be easy for me?" Kat put in. "You've always been a shadowy figure in my life, all my life. You were rarely there. A sister who wasn't even a sister. I used to make excuses because there was such an age difference between us. So what makes you think I want to change anything either? We haven't even so much as spoken for over a year."

"I know. And I am genuinely sorry about that. But you'll have to admit that's not entirely my fault. You've never contacted me either."

Kat knew this was true. "Would you have wanted me to?"

Beth didn't reply for long moments. "I have to say on some level I've regretted that we couldn't be closer. I know we should have been. But I could also see it would have been complicated."

"Did Mum tell you that?" Kat asked sharply and Beth paused again.

"I don't think so. Not in so many words. After you were born Mum said it would be best if I didn't get involved with you. She decided I should stay on with Aunt Grace for a few months. By the time I came home everything was in place. Mum was Mum, you were the new baby and I was the big sister. Mum and Dad went back to being parents, and I went back to school."

Kat was amazed. Her mother's elder sister, their Aunt Grace, was even more self-possessed and introverted than her mother was. Kat couldn't remember Aunt Grace being at all interested in either of them, Beth or Kat. "Aunt Grace was part of it?"

"No." Beth shook her head. "As far as I know Mum and Dad, and the doctor of course, were the only ones who knew. Mum told Aunt Grace she just needed to get used to having another baby without having the complications of me around. So I stayed with her. Aunt Grace's only comment was that she found it extremely distasteful that Mum and Dad were doing that sort of thing at their age."

Kat gave a reluctant smile. That rang true. "It can't have been easy for you," she said, surprising herself.

"I suppose not. I think I've put it all out of my mind for so long it seems like someone else's dream."

They lapsed into silence again.

"Mum should never have done it," Kat said at last.

"I know. But she did. And we can't change that. In her strange way she probably thought she was doing the right thing."

"That's what Dad said the other night." *When my world was knocked off its axis*, Kat thought to herself.

"So. As they say, what's done is done," Beth said almost matter-of-factly. "And it begs the question, where do we go from here?"

"You said before you didn't want any upheavals in your life," Kat reminded her.

"That's not quite what I said."

"As good as."

"I'm trying to be honest with you, Kat. I simply don't think I'm ready, if I'll ever be ready, to change our roles. And I don't think you want to either."

"You don't know what I think." Kat knew she sounded petulant but couldn't seem to stop herself. "About this or anything else for that matter, wouldn't you say?"

"That's probably a fair comment," Beth agreed graciously. "So. Maybe we could do something about that."

"About what exactly?"

"About us. About each other. Maybe we could talk more often, get to know each other better."

"We do know each other," Kat said, knowing nothing could be further from the truth.

"Do we?" Beth raised one dark eyebrow. "What do you think you know about me?"

Kat shrugged. "I know you were pregnant at sixteen." Kat took herself to task and made herself meet Beth halfway. "You did well at school, which was probably amazing considering. You worked hard at your job, and now you own your own company. And you got married eleven years ago. None of us attended the wedding."

"And so passed over thirty years." Beth smiled faintly. "Yes to all you mentioned. But with hindsight I know I tended to keep the most significant areas of my life well distant from you and Mum and Dad."

"What do you mean?"

"I sometimes feel I existed in parallel universes to some extent. There was my family life and my true reality. For instance, most significantly, did you know I had an on-again-off-again relationship with an older and very much married man for twenty years or so?"

Kat gazed across at Beth in surprise. "You did?"

"I did. And he was my boss."

Kat tried to read behind Beth's closed expression but could only detect a calm acceptance. "And Mum didn't know?"

Beth laughed softly then. "What do you think?"

"I'd say that would be a no. If Mum had known it would have been just one more dissatisfaction she could have used to verbally abuse Dad with."

Beth glanced down at her hands. "I guess you're right. Anyway, I never told her. Yet he was an important part of my life for a very long time."

Kat tried to recall all she knew about Beth's boss. He was the previous owner of Beth's company, and she had known he was married with a family. She remembered her mother often complaining about Beth working such long hours. She'd also got the impression that Beth's boss's wife was from what her mother referred to as old money, and more than once she'd shown Kat photos in the newspaper of the couple attending some function or other. She held Beth's gaze again. "Were you in love with him?"

"Perhaps. I thought I was for a long time."

"Did his wife ever, well, know about you and him?"

Beth shook her head. "I don't think so. He always said he'd leave her when his children grew up." She gave a bitter laugh.

"Saying that out loud makes me seem very gullible, doesn't it?"

"But he never left her?"

"No. But who knows. It never came to that. Fate stepped in. His wife was involved in an awful car accident and was, still is, confined to a wheelchair. He became remorseful and decided to sell the business so he could care for her. I decided I'd buy it and because he was so remorseful I was able to afford it. A couple of years later I met Phil."

There was silence again while Kat digested all that Beth had said.

"All that, well, the last bit, is in confidence, of course."

"Off the record?" Kat said wryly.

"If you like. So, what about you?" Beth prompted.

"What about me?" Even as she said the words Kat was overcome by guilt again. She reminded herself again that she was supposed to be meeting Beth halfway. She shrugged. "Not much to tell. I still teach at the same school, and I'm renovating this house."

"Short and to the point," Beth remarked. "Em tells me you and Shael broke up."

Kat's eyebrows rose in surprise. She had never discussed her sexuality with Beth, but it seemed Em had. Something else Em hadn't mentioned, apparently. "Oh, yes. I forgot," Kat said off-handedly. "And I'm a lesbian. But it seems you already know that."

"Yes, I know you are. I've known since Mum told me all about you and Ruth Dunleavy."

"She told you?" Kat rolled her eyes. "Why am I not surprised?"

"She wanted me to talk to you, to try to, as she put it, talk some sense into you."

"She did?"

"She did." Beth laughed softly. "Which is quite amusing on a number of fronts, not the least that I didn't think I had any right to try to tell you anything, but especially how to live your life. Actually, I knew Ruth."

Kat looked at Beth in amazement. Yet she shouldn't be

surprised. They were almost the same age and grew up in the same suburb.

"I didn't know her well," Beth continued, "but we were both keen golfers at one stage and belonged to the same golf club. I quite liked her. She was bright and entertaining. She made no secret of the fact she was a lesbian even then."

"You weren't—" Kat tried to choose her words carefully. "You never thought you might be a lesbian, too?"

Beth was momentarily taken aback. "No. Why would you think that? Because I knew Ruth?"

Kat shrugged. "Ruth didn't have many straight friends. You only seemed to mix with women, and you didn't get married until you were almost forty."

"I was with Ben for most of those years. Secretly." Beth gave a crooked smile. "I suppose it was akin to being in the closet. But no, I wasn't a lesbian. I simply wasted too many years on a lost cause."

Their eyes met again and Beth sighed. "But part of me can well and truly understand why you shied off men."

"That's not what I did," Kat said emphatically. "I simply prefer women."

"All right. So you prefer women," Beth placated. "All I wanted to say was that unlike Mum and Dad, I have no problem with that. It's your preference. And I would never presume to try to tell you how to live your life. I certainly didn't let anyone tell me how to live mine." She paused. "Well, after you were born, that is."

Kat sat silently digesting Beth's words. She supposed she should be grateful Beth didn't subscribe to their parents' opinions on Kat's supposedly abhorrent lifestyle.

"I just wanted to know if you were okay," Beth repeated and Kat looked up inquiringly. "I mean, apart from the shock of Mum's revelations, are you getting over your breakup with Shael? Em said you'd been together for ten years."

Kat paused. Just short weeks ago she would have said she felt she'd never get over Shael's betrayal. But now, with this change of scene and a new focus, she knew she was getting her life back together. The heavy depression she'd felt in the awful old flat had lifted and if it hadn't been for Meggie, Kat knew she could simply have moved on with her new life. But there was Meggie. There always would be Meggie. Kat loved her dearly and would never be able to walk away from her.

"I see you aren't over her." Beth's soft words drew Kat back from her thoughts.

"Oh, no. I mean, yes, I am. I'm okay. I'll admit I was devastated in the beginning, and I'm still sort of upset but not in the same way. We, Shael and I, just have to sort things out. Financially. And about Meggie."

"Meggie?" Beth frowned, obviously puzzled.

"Yes. Em didn't mention her?"

"No. I don't think she did."

"Now, that's very unlike Em, the news of the world."

Beth smiled. "I suppose so. Em's very, well, open. No, she didn't tell me about Meggie. Was she the other woman involved?"

"No." Kat shook her head. "Meggie's ten going on thirty, and she's," she shrugged, "I guess she's sort of your granddaughter."

"You had a child?" Beth asked incredulously.

"Meggie's not my biological daughter. I wish she was. She was just a baby when Shael and I met. But I couldn't love her more if she was my daughter."

"Well, I'm totally surprised. I mean, I knew you and Ruth broke up, and I knew you were with Shael. I think you even mentioned her once or twice when we spoke."

"On the rare occasions we spoke."

Beth nodded. "We should have contacted each other more often, I know. I suppose we're both products of our upbringing. If we had spoken at least I'd have known about Meggie, wouldn't I?"

Kat knew it was as much her fault as Beth's and she said as much. "I'm sorry. I should have made more of an effort."

"We both should." She paused. "Maybe sometime you could introduce me to Meggie."

Slowly Kat smiled. "I'd like that. You'll love her."

Beth glanced at the time. "I guess I should go now. I said I'd take Dad up to the hospital." She slid a glance at Kat. "I don't suppose you want to come with us."

Emotions rose and warred inside Kat. "I don't think I can," she said at last. "I'm sorry, Beth. I'm not ready. Not just yet."

"All right. I understand." She walked to the door and Kat followed her. "I will keep in touch though, Kat. I promise." And then she was gone, leaving Kat with even more to think about.

Kat washed her dishes after eating a light dinner she hadn't tasted. Her mind went from Beth to her unknown biological father then to Jess as she relived pieces of conversations, of memories. But mostly she thought of Jess and those stolen moments she wished had gone on forever. Her emotions felt like they were running on a never-ending roller coaster.

Finally, in exasperation, she had a long shower before donning comfortable old baggy shorts and an equally old T-shirt. She was about to sit down and check out what was on television when there was a tentative knock on her door. Kat opened it to find a subdued Jess standing there.

"Can I come in?" Jess asked formally.

CHAPTER EIGHT

"Of course." Kat stood back.

Jess wore a pair of faded denim jeans and a black sleeveless tank top that molded to her breasts and her flat stomach. Kat's senses went into overdrive again, that same desire rising inside her, and she bit back a moan. "Sit down," she offered, her voice almost steady.

"No. Thanks." Jess thrust her hands in the pockets of her jeans. "I just called in because I thought we should talk. About yesterday." Her gaze went to the hallway leading to Kat's bedroom and just as quickly slid away. She took a deep breath. "Firstly, I think I should apologize for my unprofessional behavior. I don't usually, well—"

"It's okay," Kat said quickly. "Don't worry about it." Her heart constricted in her chest. Obviously, Jess thought it was a mistake. Why had Kat allowed herself to think otherwise? "I can forget it ever happened," she added, amazed at her capacity to lie. *Tell me not to forget*, she silently pleaded with Jess.

"Oh." Jess seemed to be finding the tips of her sandals fascinating. "That's good of you." She looked back at Kat and away again. "Because I don't do that sort of thing. Make passes at clients. Male or female. I can't explain my lapse in judgment. I just—" Her gaze met Kat's, and this time she didn't look away.

Kat was sure she could see a jumble of conflicting emotions reflected there. Fear, definitely. And desire. Kat recognized it because she felt that same heady hunger. She stepped closer to Jess and Jess amazingly held her ground.

"I wasn't offended," Kat said carefully. "Quite the contrary."

Jess's laugh sounded a little forced. "So you're used to, well, that?"

"No. It was a first actually." Kat gave a crooked smile.

"For me, too," Jess got out thickly.

They stood there looking at each other, and it seemed to Kat the silence enveloped them, keeping them captive. Time stood still, the universe holding its breath. Then a dull flush rose in Jess's cheeks.

"I—" Her gaze moved over Kat's body, settled on the rise of her breasts beneath the old T-shirt, and Kat's body responded spontaneously. Slowly, Jess reached out and ran her fingertips over the swell of one of Kat's breasts, reaching the taut peak.

Kat could barely breathe as pure sensation rose to completely engulf her. Her nerve endings sent pulses racing inside her, rising in a crescendo of desire. She felt exhilarated yet slightly lightheaded, and a low emotive moan escaped from deep in her chest.

Jess's tongue tip dampened her lips. "I couldn't keep away," she said hoarsely and swallowed, her pulse beating wildly, erratically.

They moved into each other, lips, breasts, stomachs, thighs melting together. Their hands explored, caressed, teased feverishly. Kat held Jess close, feeling the sensation of standing poised on a precipice, in grave danger of tumbling into the unknown. Her T-shirt was discarded on the floor with Jess's tank top and bra and when Kat pulled open the press-stud at the waist of Jess's jeans, the sound seemed to explode about them.

Kat paused, her eyes meeting Jess's, pleading an unspoken question.

Jess swallowed again, her lips swollen from Kat's kisses, her eyes dark and desire-filled. She took Kat's hand, moving them past the kitchen, into Kat's darkened bedroom.

Kat felt around and flicked on the bedside lamp tossing pools of shadowy light about them. She threw back the bedspread, then turned back to Jess. Jess had stepped out of her jeans, and she reached out to slide Kat's shorts down over her hips so they slipped to the floor. She reached for Kat, and they fell on the bed in a tangle of naked arms and legs, skin to burning skin.

Entranced, Kat ran her fingers over Jess's body, her throat, her breasts, over the flat of her midriff, her stomach, then beneath the thin, silky material of her underpants. Jess pushed her undies down, wriggled out of them and her hand covered Kat's, guiding it to her hair-covered mound. Kat rested her hand there for long moments as she kissed Jess's breasts, her mouth settling around one nipple. And then her fingers found Jess's centre.

Jess clutched Kat to her as she exploded into orgasm, and Kat held her close until Jess caught her breath. Then she felt Jess's lips on her own body, her fingers seeking Kat's sensitive places. Kat shifted her position slightly to thrust her pelvis against Jess's hand, subtly giving Jess her rhythm. Moments later Kat cascaded into her own orgasm.

They clung together, both lingering in the elated aftermath of release. Jess's lips playfully encircled Kat's breast, kissing and suckling, and they moved together again, lips sliding, fingertips seeking and finding, until they were both spent.

With Jess clinging to her, Kat flicked off the lamp and drifted off to sleep, so aware of the steady beat of Jess's heart. Jess in her arms, Kat thought euphorically, where Kat knew she was meant to be.

The sound of a phone woke them. Slowly, disorientated, they both peered into the darkness.

"Mine, I think," said Jess sleepily. She leaned over the side of the bed and fumbled in the pocket of her discarded jeans. She checked the number and sat up on her elbow. "Miranda? Is something wrong?" She frowned. "You mean he's physically throwing up? Where's Dad? All right."

She slid a glance at Kat and Kat reached out, cupping one of Jess's naked breasts in her hand. A tremor ran through Jess. She closed her eyes then opened them and glanced at Kat. "I'm over at Kat's place," she told her daughter. "But I was just about to head off home. We got talking and lost track of the time." Jess stopped and grimaced. "I'll be home soon, love. Okay. 'Bye."

Jess rang off. "I have to go," she told Kat quickly. "The dog's sick again." She fiddled with the mobile, not meeting Kat's gaze. "Lucas isn't home from his meeting and Mark's asleep. I have to get back."

"I know," Kat said reluctantly.

"I'm sorry." Jess slid out of bed.

The lamplight highlighted the shape of her body, the shaded lines of its wonderful curves, and Kat groaned regretfully. "I'm sorry, too. Really, really sorry," she added softly as she stretched her aching muscles.

Jess watched her, her expression unreadable in the shadowy light. She pulled on her undies and jeans, looked about for her bra and top before remembering they were in the living room. She walked down the hallway.

Naked, Kat followed her.

Jess pulled on her tank top and turned back to Kat just as Kat went to retrieve her own discarded T-shirt. Before she could slip it over her head, Jess pulled her into her arms. She kissed Kat thoroughly, deeply, a long drugging kiss, then released her and headed for the door.

"Night," she said huskily as she left.

Kat stood there until she heard the sound of Jess's car disappear into the darkness.

The sound of Tom Worrall next door busily mowing his lawn woke Kat the next morning. She glanced at the bedside clock in amazement. It was after ten o'clock. She'd well and truly overslept. Which wasn't all that surprising really after the emotional day she'd had, first with Beth, then those wonderful, incredible hours she'd spent with Jess.

Kat stretched languidly and tried to wipe the smile off her face. She clutched the other pillow to her, breathing in Jess's scent. Proof, she told herself, that she hadn't been dreaming, that Jess had been here in Kat's bed and that they'd made amazing, incredible love.

Reluctantly she got out of bed and headed for the shower. She made herself a late breakfast and ate hungrily, acknowledging that she hadn't felt so alive in years.

And then niggling doubts began to set in. Jess had left hurriedly. But she'd kissed Kat goodbye, she reminded herself. Yet she couldn't prevent herself from wondering if Jess would want to come back.

Positives and negatives raged inside Kat as she tried to get more work done on the house. Eventually, she told herself that if Jess didn't call her by dinnertime, she'd call her. Simple. Decision made. And she set to preparing the second bathroom for the tradesmen who were scheduled to arrive in a couple of days.

A few hours later someone knocked on her door, and she felt herself begin to smile. She wiped her hands and walked through to the living room.

Kat opened the door, Jess in her thoughts, as she seemed to have been forever. She was still smiling. Her mind flashed images from the night before intermingled with the here and now. It didn't take much of a stretch of her vivid imagination to see herself pulling Jess back into her arms, burying herself in Jess, the soft, tropical fruit smell of her shampoo, the taste of her skin.

But it wasn't Jess and Kat felt her smile fade. To her surprise Shael stood there in the light cascading onto the veranda from the hot summer sun. One dark eyebrow climbed sardonically, and she inclined her head, her dark hair shimmering in the light. "Hello, Kat."

"Shael? Hello." Kat glanced past her ex-partner, expecting to see Meggie there behind her. "Is Meggie with you? Is she all right?" Concern rose inside Kat. Why else would Shael be here?

"No, she's not with me. And yes, she's fine," Shael said pleasantly enough. "She's gone shopping with Mum and Dad. So. Can I come in?"

Kat hesitated and then reluctantly stood back. What could Shael want? For her to drive all this way Kat could only think from past experience that it probably wouldn't bode well for Kat. She couldn't prevent herself from checking Shael's car parked at the curb on the other side of the road, but she couldn't see any sign of Tori.

"I came alone." Shael grimaced. "Tori's not with me if that's what you're concerned about."

Kat made no comment as Shael stepped into the living room and looked around. "I thought Meggie said you didn't have furniture."

Kat shrugged. "I didn't. In the beginning. Second-hand shops were handy."

Shael frowned slightly. "You know if you want money you just have to ask. And you can have any of the furniture at home if you want it."

"Thanks. But I'm fine. I'll give it some thought though." Kat bit her lip. "That's not what you said before, when I moved out."

Shael made an irritated movement with her hand. "Things were heated. The situation wasn't ideal. We were angry."

"Oh. As I seem to recall it, you were angry. I was—" Kat shook her head. What had she been? Stunned? Even though she suspected Shael was having an affair, yes, she'd been stunned. Disappointed? That, too. Disappointed that Shael had betrayed her yet again.

"Kat." Shael took a step closer, smiled the smile that had first attracted Kat. "Let's forget all that, put it behind us. We can't live in the past. It's not healthy."

Where was all this heading? Kat knew Shael of old. She

had to have an agenda. Otherwise why was she here? All Kat's instincts told her to show Shael to the door, and she would have, if it hadn't been for Meggie.

"How about some coffee?" Shael suggested easily. "I had a quick bite to eat before I left the hospital, but I didn't stop for coffee."

Kat paused again. She knew she should open some dialogue with Shael about the house and their shared assets, but all she really wanted was to discuss Meggie, and she knew she'd have to step cautiously there.

"I won't bite, you know."

Kat looked up in surprise to see Shael had stepped even closer to her.

"I never have, have I? Bitten you, I mean." Shael gave a crooked smile. "Not unless you asked me to."

Kat swallowed, her face coloring. Shael was obviously confusing her with one of her other women. "You know I'm not into that." She had a sudden flash from last night of her nibbling tantalizing little bites downwards, over the smooth skin of Jess's midriff, her stomach. And she gave a soft cough.

Shael laughed. "I know you weren't. I was just teasing you. You always look so cute when you're being oh-so-proper."

"Shael, what do you want?"

"Megghan talks constantly about your renovations. I thought I'd come and see for myself."

Kat didn't believe that for a minute. Past experience had taught her that.

"So, it seems like the work's well under way." Shael looked up at the now uncovered pressed metal ceiling but made no comment about it. "Aren't you going to show me around?"

Kat made no move to give her a grand tour but she reluctantly told her about the plans she had for the house.

"Impressive." Shael moved across the room towards the breakfast bar. "I have to say it looks good so far. It will certainly add to the price of the place. So do I get coffee?" she asked, turning her best smile on for Kat.

Perhaps Shael had just come to check the house was a reasonable environment for Meggie. No matter what Kat thought of Shael regarding their relationship, she couldn't deny Shael was a good mother to Meggie. Kat decided she could be misjudging Shael. She relaxed a little and went into the kitchen. "I've only got instant coffee," she said as she set the kettle boiling.

"That will be fine." Uninvited, Shael moved about the house. When she stood in the doorway of the bedroom and looked inside Kat tensed, her nerves and her emotions skittering about in a jumble of mixed sensations from the past and the present. She took a deep breath, not wanting to give Shael anything to hone in on about her life here and now. Kat knew Shael was a past master at relegating Kat's life, her hopes, her dreams, to the inconsequential. Kat had no intentions of allowing Shael to negate her life now. Not her work on the house. And definitely not her feelings for Jess Andrews. Because she knew Shael was capable of doing just that with a word.

Yet, it hadn't always been so. In the beginning they had been friends. In the beginning Kat would have told her about her growing love for transforming this old house. And she would have told her about the upheaval in her life finding out that Beth was her biological mother. But not now. "White. No sugar. Right?" she said as evenly as she could.

Shael rejoined her in the kitchen. "How could you forget?" she asked, her voice low.

Kat made no comment. She simply handed Shael her coffee before picking up her own cup and indicating that they return to the living room. She sat down in a chair and waited while Shael sat opposite her.

Shael took a sip of coffee. "Mmm. Just the way I like it. You always could make a great cup of coffee."

Kat shrugged. "Anyone can pour hot water onto a spoonful of coffee granules," she remarked dryly. That would be a point to me, she said to herself, watching Shael's eyebrows rise in acknowledgment. However, the other woman made no comment.

"So how have you been?" Shael deftly changed the subject.

Kat looked across at her in surprise. Was Shael genuinely interested? And why now? "I'm fine," she said carefully. *Basically, I'm over you*, Kat wanted to add, but what would be the point. It would only be more ammunition for Shael and as far as Kat was concerned, that particular war was over.

"So who's this Jess Megghan can't stop talking about?"

Ah, was this the point of Shael's visit? If so, it begged the question why did Shael care. Kat pulled herself together. She was in a quandary trying to analyse everything Shael said. Was she reading far more into her questions and her motives? Shael had been the one who called off their relationship. It might just be innocent curiosity on Shael's part. Yet the latter part of their relationship made it difficult for Kat not to consider underlying angles.

"Jess? She's Miranda's mother," she said with as much composure as she could muster, considering just the mention of Jess's name changed Kat's entire focus. Her heart beat faster, rising in her throat. Her mouth went dry. Her lips softened anticipating Jess's kiss. A spiral of wanting teased the pit of her stomach. And her fingers tingled just to have Jess there so she could reach out and touch her.

"Oh, yes. Miranda." Shael nodded. "Megghan's new friend."

"She's in the cricket team Meggie's just joined. Jess is one of the coaches."

"And I spoke to her? When I was in Sydney. That was Jess?"

"Yes." Kat nodded.

"So you met Miranda and Jess at cricket?"

"Well, no." Kat could have bitten her tongue. Why did she have to be so candid? She should have left it at that. It was far too dangerous to discuss Jess with Shael. "She owns the company doing my house renovations," Kat added quickly.

"I see." Shael gave a knowing smile. "Don't you just love a woman with power tools?"

"She doesn't do the hands-on stuff." Even as she said it Kat had a flash of memory from the night before, Jess's hands moving on her body, and she felt herself flush. "She handles the office side of the business. Her husband and her cousin run the actual building section."

"Oh." Shael's eyebrows shot up again. "She's married then?"

Kat knew she should tell Shael that Jess and Mark were divorced, but this time she resisted the urge to comment.

"Well, you know what they say about married women. Far too complicated."

"Shael, I don't understand where this is going?" Kat decided she'd had enough of whatever game Shael was playing.

"I can't simply just be concerned about you?" Shael appealed innocently.

"There's no need for your concern. I told you I was fine and I am."

Shael held Kat's gaze and Kat made herself remain calm and outwardly relaxed. "You haven't asked about me?" Shael said at last, momentarily disconcerting Kat, and she paused again before replying.

"Then how are you?" she asked at last.

"Not as fine as you are. Apparently," Shael added wryly. She set her mug on the coffee table and stood up, crossed the room to stand gazing out the window. "Tori's left me," she said flatly.

"She has?" Kat stood up too. "I'm sorry to hear that."

"Are you? Really, I mean?" Shael gave a soft laugh and turned to face Kat. "And you don't want to say, I told you so?"

"No. I don't." Kat realized it was the truth. What would be the point? She'd moved on. And she knew she wouldn't have said it anyway. It wasn't her style. "And I do mean that. I'm sorry it didn't work out."

"Yes." Shael gave a crooked smile. "But I wouldn't blame you if you did say it, because you did warn me, didn't you?"

Kat continued to offer no comment.

"Ah, Kat." Shael shook her head. "I don't know why I want you to give me the satisfaction of hearing you say it. You never were the malicious type, were you? That was strictly my department."

"What happened?" Kat asked, and Shael gave that same rueful smile.

"Another woman. What else?" She laughed shortly. "You know, I've always considered myself to be reasonably intelligent, but I think it's time I admitted I can be a trifle dense when it comes to relationships, and more specifically, to specific women. Wouldn't you say, Kat?"

Kat agreed wholeheartedly but didn't say so. For Shael to be on the receiving end of infidelity and rejection should be enough of a blow to her self-esteem. Kat had no desire to get involved in Shael's apparent enlightened moment.

"I guess I got bowled over by her allure." Shael shrugged. "But that's no excuse, is it? I should have sorted out you and me before I got involved with Tori, shouldn't I?"

"Yes, but that's easy to say with hindsight."

"And that's generous of you Kat. Really," she added at Kat's skeptical look. Shael walked over to the door, restless now, then she turned back to face Kat. "Look, I could say so many things to you, Kat, but I know it wouldn't make up for what I've put you through over the years." She came closer till she was standing in front of Kat and took her hand. "Can you see yourself forgiving me?" she asked huskily.

Kat looked into her eyes. "If that's what you want, Shael. I do. I have. If it helps I've put it all behind me, made a new life. Who knows, maybe we can find some level of friendship."

"Thanks, Kat." Shael leaned forward, kissed Kat on the cheek, and then her arms reached out, pulled Kat against her, into her arms. Before Kat could react, Shael's mouth found hers.

Kat was completely dumbfounded. Never in a million years would she have surmised that was Shael's intention. Kat seemed paralysed, her body unable to respond in any way. Only when the intensity of Shael's kiss subtly changed did Kat's body come to life. She pushed against Shael, put some small distance between them, holding herself as far away as Shael's encircling arms would allow.

"I really do love you, Kat," Shael said earnestly. "I always have."

"Shael, I—" At that moment a movement behind Shael caught Kat's attention.

Jess stood in the doorway behind Shael, backlit by the brightness of the outside sunlight, her expression unreadable in the shadow.

CHAPTER NINE

"Oh. Jess." Kat pushed against Shael's hold again, and Shael slowly released her. "Jess, I—"

Jess moved then. "I'm so sorry," she said stiltedly. "I didn't realize you had visitors. I didn't mean to interrupt. I was just checking up on"—she swallowed—"on the kitchen installation."

Kat blinked. "The kitchen? Oh, yes. They finished it on Monday." Jess knew that.

"Good." Jess nodded. "I'll make a note of that. Well, I'll catch up with you later, Kat."

By the time Kat could move Jess had gone. Kat was galvanized into action. She raced out the door and down the stairs. She reached Jess's van just as Jess started the engine. "Jess. Wait." Kat rapped on the closed window.

After a moment Jess reached out and pushed a button to slide the window down.

"Jess." Kat's mouth went dry.

"It's okay, Kat," Jess said, not quite meeting Kat's eyes. "I should have phoned before I came over."

"No. You can call in anytime," Kat said quickly.

Jess gave a small, crooked smile. "But just not right now."

"Jess, it wasn't what—"

"What it looked like?" Jess finished. "Who is she?"

"It's Shael. Meggie's mother."

"I see." Jess nodded.

"No, you don't. I… we…"

"You're old friends. I know. You told me."

"We are," Kat began.

"Kat!" Shael called down from the veranda. "Megghan wants to talk to you." She held up Kat's phone.

"I have to go," Jess said. "I have a couple of quotes to do. I'll see you later."

The car began to move, and Kat could only step back and watch Jess drive away. After long moments staring at the spot where Jess had been, Kat turned and walked back up the steps. Wordlessly she took the phone from Shael. "Meggie?" Kat was half expecting the line to be empty but Meggie answered brightly.

"Hi, Kat. Mum said she was visiting you and you were talking to Jess. Did you say hi for me?"

"Yes. Look, Meggs, I can't talk right now. Was it important?"

"Not exactly. I just wanted to talk to you."

"And I want to talk to you, too. Anytime. But there's something I need to discuss with your mother. How about if I ring you back in a little while."

"Sure, Kat." There was a small pause. "You aren't fighting, are you? You and Mum, I mean. Because I think Tori's left. I noticed her gear was gone when Gran dropped me over to get my iPod I forgot to take with me."

"I know, love. We'll talk soon. Okay?"

"Okay. 'Bye, Kat."

Kat hung up and turned back to Shael.

"Something tells me there's more to all this than meets the proverbial eye," Shael said, standing regarding Kat, her arms folded easily.

Kat just stood there, her mind spinning a kaleidoscope of thoughts in her head, and she seemed to be incapable of clutching at any of them. She could feel her heart racing in her chest and she swallowed, trying to calm herself. Jess couldn't be thinking last night had meant so little to Kat that she'd be romancing her ex-partner today, could she?

"Come on, Kat," Shael cajoled. "Tell all."

"There's nothing to tell."

"No? I'm positive there is." Shael pursed her lips. "The signs are flashing red."

"What signs? I told you there's nothing to tell."

"Well, you must be pretty perturbed about something. You fobbed Megghan off. I don't think I remember you doing that before. Ever."

"I didn't fob her off I just—I'm going to ring her back."

Shael continued to regard Kat speculatively. "All right. Then what do you think about my idea?"

"What idea?" Kat asked distractedly. She was struggling to concentrate on Shael. All she could see was the shock on Jess's face for that split second before she got herself under control.

"About us."

"Us?" Kat blinked. She was hearing Shael's words but they weren't computing.

"Yes, well, I'll admit I hadn't got past the kiss before we were rudely interrupted. Total bad timing."

Kat frowned. "Shael, what are you trying to say?"

"What do you think I'm saying? I mean, maybe we should get back together. Give it another try. We were good together. We could be again."

"I don't think that would be a good idea," Kat replied flatly. Her whole body was numb. She knew she should be reacting to the ridiculousness of Shael's proposition, but her emotions were in shutdown mode.

"Why not? It would be right on any number of levels. We wouldn't have the upheaval of sorting out our affairs. You can sell this old place, move back home. We could put the pool in you always wanted. I know Megghan would think it was a fantastic idea."

"Meggie?" Was Shael dangling Meggie in front of Kat like bait on a hook? Suddenly an icy anger enveloped Kat and she lost control. Shael went to say more but Kat held up her hand. "No. Don't! Don't say another word, Shael. I think you'd better leave. Now!"

"Kat, come on," Shael coaxed softly. "I know I've made mistakes. Hell, I knew Tori was a mistake a week after she moved in. But you and I, Kat, we have history. I think we're meant to be together. With Megghan."

"How could I be so blind?" Kat said coldly. "Why didn't I see just how shallow you really are? Surely you couldn't have always been like this? In the beginning?"

"Look, Kat. I've told you I've made mistakes. Everybody does. Even you."

"I know I have. But I've always been upfront with you." Kat shook her head in exasperation. "I've never cheated or lied to you, Shael."

"Oh, for heaven's sake, Kat. Don't go all holier-than-thou on me. You don't know what it's like in the real world. These women, they make themselves so available. I'm only human."

"You'd better go. Please."

They stood for long moments just glaring at each other.

"Is it that woman?" Shael asked. "Jess?"

"I don't think that's any of your business anymore."

Shael gave a short laugh. "You said she was married, Kat. At least I didn't get involved with the married ones. That sort of situation can explode in your face. You know how it can be with straight women. Things are probably a bit jaded at home, and she's out looking to experiment on the wild side. Knowing you, I can't see that being any good for your soft heart and tender sensitivities."

"Jess is divorced," Kat said before she could stop herself. "And I'm not going to discuss Jess with you, Shael, so I'd like you to leave. I have nothing more to say to you."

"Not even about Megghan?"

Kat stilled, an icy hand wrapping around her heart.

"About how often you see her?"

Kat swallowed and then drew herself up to her full height. She held Shael's gaze and Shael's was the first to fall. "Even you wouldn't stoop so low as to use Meggie against me, would you, Shael?"

"I'm her mother—"

"Then act like her mother and think about what you're doing to her."

"Legally, the decisions regarding Megghan are mine."

"Meggie loves you, Shael. Only you know if you're capable of manipulating that love. Now, please leave. Do what you have to do to me, but don't take it out on Meggie."

Shael stood there for long seconds before she turned and left.

Kat didn't watch her go. She crossed the room, picked up the phone and dialed Jess's office number. Jess was out of the office, Jeanne told her, but she gave Kat Jess's mobile number. Kat rang it but only got the message bank. She couldn't leave a message. She didn't know what to say to make it right.

For long, tortured moments Kat simply sat there before making her promised call to Meggie. Kat made herself listen as Meggie told her all about a visit to Australia Zoo. Her grandparents had been promising to take her, and they'd gone the day before.

"And the crocodiles were awesome, Kat. Really scary. And there were stacks of other animals too."

"Sounds like you had fun."

"I did. But I wish Miranda had been able to come. Mum said it would be better if Gran and Grandpa only had me to worry about. Have you seen Jess?"

"Jess? Ah, yes. She called in earlier, but she was pretty busy."

"Oh. I guess she must be. Miranda says they all work pretty hard. Like Mum does, I guess."

"Mmm."

"Is something wrong, Kat? You're a bit, well, distracted or something."

"No. I'm fine, love. What else did you do at Gran's?"

"Only Australia Zoo. And shopping." Meggie paused. "So what did Mum want? What did you talk about?"

Kat tried to keep her voice even. "Oh, not much, really."

"Did she tell you she broke up with Tori?"

"Yes. She told me."

"I don't suppose you'd come back now, would you, Kat?" Meggie asked in a strained voice.

"Oh, Meggs. You know I can't do that."

Meggie sighed. "I know that, I guess. You and Mum don't love each other anymore, hey?"

"But we both love you. You know that, don't you?"

"Yep. I just wish that you, like, maybe lived next door so I could see you whenever I wanted to."

"I'd like that too. But I have to finish fixing up this house."

"And I guess Mr. and Mrs. Thomas and Mr. Gardham don't really want to sell the houses next door. And I don't think Mum wants to move house either."

"So that means we make the most of the time we do get to see each other, doesn't it?"

"I suppose." Meggie sighed again. "And I'm still coming over at the weekend, aren't I? Because Miranda said they need me to play in the cricket team. Can you remind Mum, Kat?"

"I don't think there'll be a problem." Kat fervently hoped there wouldn't be.

"Maybe I'll ask Mum if she wants to come and watch me play. Then she can meet Miranda and Jess and Caleb."

"I suppose it will depend on her work schedule."

"Okay. But I can ask her. I have to go now, Kat. We're going down to see Aunty Angela. I'll be missing you until the weekend. 'Bye."

"Me too. 'Bye."

Kat hung up and tears ran down her cheeks. Eventually, she pulled herself together. She went into the bathroom, not looking at the bed, wanting no memories of Jess last night just at that moment. She glanced in the mirror, grimacing at her red eyes and nose and blotchy skin. She splashed her face with water and ran a comb through her hair. And she stood there, looking at her reflection.

So what should she do now? Her first priority was to explain everything to Jess. But who could blame Jess if she didn't want it made right. Allowing that she'd ever wanted it made right at all, of course.

Kat swallowed the lump that rose in her throat. She didn't really know what Jess wanted. What if Shael was right and Jess just wanted to experiment. Kat's heart sank. Had she been expecting Jess would want an honest relationship? Of course she had. Yet it would be complicated. She knew that. Jess still lived in the family home. She had children, an ex-husband. Wouldn't deciding to live with another woman be too difficult a situation for Jess to even contemplate? The alternative was sneaking around, grabbing moments here and there to be together.

Kat asked herself what she wanted herself. She had to admit it wasn't that. She wanted more than that. So much more. She wanted Jess. Beside her. Forever. *Dream on*, her cynical inner self chided. It was more likely that Jess did just want the occasional entertaining evening. It wouldn't be worth the disruption to her ordered life. Could Kat settle for that? A tear trickled down her cheek, and she dashed it away just as her mobile phone rang.

"Kat? It's Beth."

"Oh. Hi," Kat said carefully, trying to push thoughts of Jess from her mind, and failing miserably. "Is Mum okay?"

"She's getting better each day. She has the doctors confused though. She's had every test known to man, and nothing's turned up that's conclusive. But they're letting her go home tomorrow." There was a moment of silence. "Do you think you might go and see her?"

"I don't know." Kat sighed. "Probably."

"It would be nice if you did."

"It would be nice if she accepted me for who I am too," Kat said succinctly.

"I know it would. But she has changed. Since she's been ill, I mean." It was Beth's turn to sigh. "In her own weird way she does love us, you know."

"If you say so," Kat replied dryly. "You and Dad couldn't possibly both be wrong. He said much the same thing."

"Kat, please!" Beth appealed. "She does care about us. They

both do. Anyway, that wasn't why I rang. I wanted to tell you I spoke to John Pattison. Your father."

"I see." Kat said slowly. She wasn't sure she needed any more emotional turmoil at the moment. "I thought you didn't know where he was."

"I didn't. Not until I asked his cousin, the one he was staying with back then. I'd run into her a couple of times over the years, and I knew where she worked. So I rang her."

"Did you tell her you'd been pregnant?"

"No. Of course not. I wasn't that forthcoming. I just said I'd like to catch up with him, that I had some old photographs he might like."

"And do you? Have photos, I mean."

"A couple. I… Actually, there's one I thought you might like. I was going to get it copied. Anyway, Jean gave me his phone number."

"Did you just come out and tell him about me?" Kat asked levelly, and Beth gave a short laugh.

"Not right away. But yes." She paused. "As you can imagine it wasn't the easiest of calls to make."

Kat made no comment, wanting and not wanting to hear how the conversation unfolded.

"He was a little taken aback."

Kat laughed mirthlessly. "Do you think? That would be a bit of an understatement no doubt."

"In the beginning." Beth sighed again. "He took it well, considering."

Kat gave an exclamation of disbelief.

"No. Really. After the initial shock I think he was intrigued. He wanted to know about you, what you did. We had a very positive conversation."

"And?"

"He's been divorced for five years. He has three children, all boys. One's a teacher, like you. One's a carpenter, and the youngest is going to university next year, studying marine biology." She paused. "He sounded nice, Kat."

Kat remained silent, trying to decide how she felt about all this information. She had three half-brothers? It was unbelievable.

"He wants me to give you his phone number, and he'd like you to ring him," Beth continued.

"I don't know, Beth." Kat put in hurriedly. It was all moving too quickly. "I haven't had time to decide if I want to make contact."

"I know. I told him that was how you felt. He said he understood. Anyway, here's his number." She read it off and Kat took it down in a daze. "If you do decide to talk to him, he said to ring him in the evening after eight thirty. He has his own boat building business down there and he often works late."

Kat stood clutching the phone, staring at the phone number.

"Will you ring him?" Beth asked softly.

Kat shrugged. "I still have to think about it."

"Well, that's wise. But I thought you should have the opportunity if you wanted to," Beth said.

"All right. Thanks." It was all Kat could manage to say and Beth rang off, giving Kat the impression she was reluctant to hang up.

Kat sank down onto the side of the bed and sat staring into space. She was in emotional overload, and her mind was having trouble functioning again. She knew she had to think but she was numb. She couldn't give anything her attention while she knew Jess was thinking badly of her. Tears tumbled down her cheeks again. She barely had them under control when a knock sounded on the door.

Jess? Had she come back? Kat raced out of the bedroom and down the hall, stopping in the living room as Em stepped in the door.

"Did you miss me, Kat? What's been happening while I was swanning around north Queensland?"

Kat burst into tears once more before moving into Em's sympathetic arms. When her tears abated the whole jumbled story came tumbling out, Kat telling Em that Beth was her biological mother. Stunned, Em sat Kat down and slid into the chair opposite her, listening as Kat told her about visiting her mother in hospital.

Kat also considered filling Em in on what had happened with Jess, but she couldn't do it. It was still too raw.

"I can't believe it," said Em later as she handed Kat the cup of tea she'd made them. "Beth was pregnant?" She shook her head in disbelief. "Good grief! How did they hide it?"

Kat shrugged and sipped the sweet tea. "Apparently no one suspected."

"Have you heard how your mother is now?" Em sat down opposite Kat again.

"Better than she was. Beth said when she rang earlier that they were letting her go home. I think they're still doing tests, but when I spoke to Dad he told me they've ruled out any heart problems." Kat pulled a face. "Maybe she just feels better getting the family secret off her chest."

"Clearing her conscience, you reckon? Well, I'd say it seems completely out of character for your mother to worry about her conscience. I used to hate the way she treated you when we were kids. But all that aside, I still don't get *why* she had to tell you now."

"I think she genuinely believed she was dying." Kat shrugged again. "Who knows?"

"You said you talked to Beth," Em said and Kat nodded. "How did she feel about you knowing?"

"She was calm, composed." Kat frowned. "Just being Beth, but"—Kat paused—"she wasn't horrified or anything."

"Maybe she was relieved," suggested Em. "It must have been awful for her over the years, knowing you were her child and not having any, well, input into any part of your life."

"I got the impression she didn't want any input. She admitted she wasn't maternal, but she did say perhaps we should get to know each other better."

"How do you feel about that?" Em asked.

Kat thought about it for a moment. "I'd like to. I've always regretted Beth and I weren't closer. Maybe now we can do something about that."

"Did she tell you who your father was?"

Kat nodded. "She said he didn't know she was pregnant and she never told him."

"Oh." Em regarded Kat thoughtfully. "Do you want him to know about you?"

"It's too late to keep it a secret now, Em." Kat shook her head. "Beth said she'd spoken to him"—Kat pulled a face—"and told him the good news. Apparently he was more surprised than upset."

"Phew!" Em exclaimed. "Not the sort of phone call I'd want to make. Did she tell you much about him?"

"He's a boat builder, divorced and it seems I have three half-brothers."

"My God!"

Kat nodded. "I can't get my head around that. He wants to talk to me, but I don't want to rush into anything without thinking about the repercussions."

"All I can say is, wow! You don't do drama by halves, do you?"

Kat had to laugh. "No. I surely don't. But enough about me. Did you enjoy your trip?"

"It was great. Pales into insignificance compared to what's been happening to you, but it's been ages since Joe and I had some special time together." Em smiled happily and they spent a few moments talking about the highlights of Em's time in the north of the State.

"And how's Meggie?" Em asked. "Actually I thought she might be with you and I'd be seeing her myself."

"I have seen her quite a bit. She's with Shael's parents until the weekend."

Em gave Kat a level look. "And? I sense a problem. There's something else you haven't told me, isn't there?"

"Oh, Em, I think I may have made a mistake with Shael. I as good as told her—" Kat swallowed. "I might have jeopardized my chances of seeing more of Meggie."

"She can't do it, love, and I hope you told her that."

"I think I did. I was so angry," Kat said worriedly. "That's the problem."

"Rubbish! You had every right to be angry. Not before time, I say. Shael needed some home truths. So what did you say that was so bad anyway?"

"Well, she called in before you came."

"You mean she came here? Why would she want to do that?" Em asked.

"I know you've never been completely sold on Shael, and I suppose I've known for a long time that your reservations weren't unfounded. I think I've just allowed the thought of losing Meggie to color my relationship with Shael. I should have left her years ago."

"Exactly!" stated Em with feeling. "So why *did* she come to see you?"

"It seems she's broken up with Tori."

"Oh, no! Kat, tell me she didn't suggest you get back together."

Kat nodded. "She said she thought we were meant to be together."

"Like you need that! She has a nerve, Kat. After all she's put you through." Em gave Kat a stern look. "You're not considering it, are you? I mean, it took so much out of you to make the break and I for one don't want to see you having to go through it again."

"No. I'm not considering it but—"

"No buts, Kat."

"There's Meggie."

"Kat, she can't use Meggie. When push comes to shove, even Shael couldn't do that, could she?"

"I hope not. Because, as I said, I didn't pull any punches when she was here before. But it wasn't just about Meggie." Kat bit her lip to hold back more tears.

"You mean there's more?"

Kat nodded, and Em leaned across and took her hand. "You'd better tell all then," she said gently.

"You see, Shael was kissing me—"

"You let her kiss you? Good grief, Kat! What were you thinking?"

"No." Kat held up her hand. "Let me finish, Em. It just happened. I had no idea she was going to do it and, well, Jess saw us," Kat finished thickly.

"Jess?" Em's eyebrows rose. "You mean Jess of the clipboard and cute little butt?"

Kat nodded.

"Okay," Em said slowly, drawing out the word, obviously

thinking about what Kat hadn't said. "So I'm thinking something else happened here while I was away, hmmm?"

"I think I'm in love with her, Em," Kat said miserably. "I mean, I know I'm in love with her."

"Good grief! I don't believe it. I go away for one short week, and your world spins on its axis. I'm speechless."

"If only!" Kat made an attempt at humor.

"Did you sleep with her?"

Kat blushed, and Em's lips pursed in surprise.

"So you did sleep with her. Kat, she's a married woman. You always said you wouldn't, well, do that. Remember?"

"She's divorced."

Em rolled her eyes. "And all this happened when?"

Kat didn't comment.

"Okay." Em grinned. "So what was it like?"

"Em, please. You know I'm not into kissing and telling."

Em's grin widened. "I know. But I live in hope one day you'll give me some juicy details." She sobered. "So now what?"

"It's complicated."

"Because she's been married, you mean?"

"Not just that."

Em shrugged. "But you say you're in love with her. Doesn't she love you?"

"I don't know. I thought last night…" Kat blushed again and held up her hand when Em went to speak. "Yes, it was last night. Yes, it was here. And yes, it was wonderful. And today she saw Shael kissing me."

"And you didn't tell her how that happened?"

"She drove off before I could."

"Then what are you doing sitting here all miserable?" Em stood up and pulled Kat to her feet. "You have to go and find her, make her understand. Tell her how you feel about her. Aren't I right?"

"But what if she doesn't feel the same about me?"

"What if she does?" Em rolled her eyes again. "When she saw Shael kissing you, how did she react? Was she jealous?"

Kat thought about the expression on Jess's face. There had been a moment. At the memory, a tiny wave of hope rose inside her. Kat tried to quash it but it stayed put. "She was embarrassed,

I think. She apologized for not phoning before calling in." Kat swallowed again. "Oh, Em, I don't think she liked it."

"Good! This is good, Kat. It will make her look at how she feels about you if she hasn't already done that."

"Em, I don't want to play any of those horrible games," Kat began.

"In that case, just tell her that." Em took Kat's cup from her hand and set it on the coffee table. "Go comb your hair and then go seek her out. I have to call in on Mum anyway. But promise me you'll ring me after you've seen Jess. I'll be waiting to hear what happens. You can tell me all. Okay?" She gave Kat a shove towards the bedroom before collecting their cups and rinsing them in the kitchen.

When Kat returned Em ran a speculative eye over her. "You look great, you know. All this butchy renovating has toned your muscles. I reckon if I was tempted to change direction I could be persuaded to give the lovely Jess a run for her money."

Kat gave a shaky laugh. "If you came to a momentous fork in your road of life, you mean?"

Em gave her a playful shove. "You're the only one with interesting forks in the road, Kat Oldfield."

"So you say." Kat's smile faded. "I don't know about this, Em. It mightn't be a good time. Jess is working. Maybe I should wait till later."

"There's no time like the present."

"I don't know where she might be."

"Don't you have her number?"

Kat nodded.

"Then ring her. Tell her to meet you wherever. Actually, preferably here."

"Here?"

"Mmm. Because beds are comfier and safer than the backseat of a car in broad daylight."

"Em!"

Em was on a roll. "And consider this, Kat. According to Oscar Wilde, the streets would be awash with horses bolting in abject terror when you two got to that stage, which I surely hope you do."

"Em, enough! And it's not just about sex anyway."

Em shook her head. "Honestly, I don't know how lesbians get together if they're all like you."

"Maybe some of them have good friends like you to point them in the right direction," Kat said dryly.

Em smiled and put Kat's arm through hers. "Walk me to the door and then get on that phone. And no chickening out on me, Kat. Promise?"

Kat paused. "I'm scared, Em. This... With Jess... It means so much to me, I'm terrified she won't... What if I make a colossal fool of myself?"

"Aren't a few moments of mortification worth suffering through for what you're going to gain?" When Kat made no comment Em pulled her close and hugged her. "As they say, no pain, no gain. You are being far too wussy, even for you, Kat, my love. But I love you anyway, absolutely." She kissed Kat on the cheek and Kat hugged her back.

"I love you, too, Em. Always."

A slight sound made them both pause before they turned towards the open door.

Jess stood, transfixed, in the doorway.

CHAPTER TEN

Em was the first to move. Before Kat could recover from her mixture of dismay and disbelief, Em had moved Jess into the living room, seated Kat and Jess, and was busily making fresh tea, all the while giving Jess an entertaining rundown on her week away in Townsville with her husband. Kat and Jess didn't need to comment even if they were capable of it. Kat knew she wasn't, but after a while she pulled herself together and slid a quick glance across at Jess. She was sitting looking as overwhelmed as Kat felt.

Jess was dressed in her tailored shorts and shirt, and Kat sensed she was studiously not meeting Kat's gaze. Kat's heart constricted. How much had Jess overheard? Kat tried to recall what they had said but she couldn't remember. Her mind was blank. But Jess had certainly seen Kat in Em's embrace, and she had to have seen Em kiss her.

Kat almost groaned. First Shael. Now Em. It would be funny if it wasn't so awful. Jess had to be thinking Kat spread herself around. And it certainly didn't make Kat look at all like good relationship material.

Relationships. Kat's heart sank again. What had made her think she was capable of another relationship anyway. All she knew about relationships was how to fail. What had she been thinking? She'd told Em in the beginning she wasn't interested, that it was all too difficult. So here was another momentous fork in the road of her life. The direction without Jess would certainly be far less complicated. But how she wished she could take the other one, the one that put her alongside Jess Andrews.

"Kat!" Em's voice brought Kat out of her reverie. "Here's your tea." She passed the cup to Kat, making sure she wasn't going to drop it. "I have to go over to see my mother," she glanced pointedly at her wristwatch, "and I'm already late, so I'll leave you to enjoy your tea."

Kat looked up then, trying to will Em to stay. But Em just smiled encouragingly at them both before leaning down and kissing Kat on the cheek again.

"I'm sure you both have lots to talk about. Timber. Nails. Stuff like that." Her smile widened. "'Bye, Kat. Phone me later. 'Bye, Jess. See you soon." Then Em was gone, closing the door pointedly behind her, and Kat and Jess were alone.

They looked across the coffee table at each other.

"I know," Jess said softly at last. "It wasn't what it looked like."

Kat cringed even though there was the shadow of a smile on Jess's lips. "It wasn't. Honestly. Em's like a sister."

"I know."

"And it really wasn't with Shael, either."

"I know that now." Jess grimaced. "At the time I think I overreacted. After last night I—" She paused, glanced at Kat and then down at her hands that held her teacup. "That's what love does to you I guess."

"Love?" Kat breathed, not allowing herself to fully believe what Jess had said.

"Yes." Jess flushed. "I love you, Kat, but—" She stopped and Kat made herself breathe.

"But what?" she asked carefully.

"But I think we…I need to talk to you about that, tell you a few things before we, well, before we make any decisions, so we can both decide what we'll do. That is, if you, well, want to continue—" She looked up at Kat, her eyes full of concern.

Kat wanted to take her in her arms, hold her close, tell her she didn't care what Jess did or didn't tell her. All she wanted to know was that Jess loved her. But she sensed Jess wasn't ready, and she was terrified Jess would leave again.

"You haven't said how you feel about this," Jess said quickly. "I know last night—" Jess swallowed.

"I do want to. Continue, I mean. And last night was wonderful," Kat said, her voice thick with emotion, and she saw a pulse flutter at the base of Jess's throat.

"Yes. It was. But it sort of frightened me."

"You have nothing to fear from me, Jess. I swear."

Jess gave a small nod. "Last night, afterwards, I just needed to get away, think it all through. I could have told Miranda to wake Mark when she rang about the dog, but I used that as an excuse. I wanted to think about how I felt about us, about what you meant to me, to my life. It's happened so suddenly, and I can understand that you probably needed to think about it as well."

Kat nodded too. "How was the dog?" she heard herself ask and Jess blinked and then gave a small smile.

"He's fine. It was a tennis ball this time, all chewed. I dread to think what he'll gulp down next. Maybe a soccer ball?" She swallowed. "I come with baggage, Kat," she said earnestly. "Lots of it."

"Everyone does, don't you think?"

Jess shook her head slightly.

"If you're talking broken relationships, then I can admit to a couple of my own, Shael included."

"I suppose I was talking about that." Jess sighed. "But I think

I should have told you a few things about my marriage before I allowed myself to get involved with you."

"Jess, you don't have to tell me anything you don't want to tell me," Kat said. "And as to involvement, well, I was involved anyway."

"You were?" The expression in Jess's eyes made Kat's heart leap because she began to hope again that Jess might want to stay. "I tried desperately to keep away," Jess continued, "after we…in your bedroom when Grace interrupted us." She bit her lip. "If Grace hadn't called in I couldn't have stopped."

"Me neither," Kat acknowledged, feeling herself flush.

"All along I'd been trying to keep it all business-as-usual in my dealings with you but I failed miserably. And it wasn't miserable." Jess's voice thickened huskily. "It was such a wonderful, terrifying mixture of exhilaration and abject agony. It hadn't happened to me before, Kat. Not like this. I kept looking for excuses to call and see you."

Kat began to smile. She couldn't help it. Jess had felt the same as she did.

Jess gave a soft moan. "Please, Kat. Don't look at me like that. I have to talk to you before…I want you to know, well, how things are and have been with my life."

"Nothing you could say would change how I feel about you, Jess," Kat reassured her but Jess didn't look convinced. Maybe Kat should simply kiss her. She desperately wanted to. But something told her Jess needed to talk.

"Last night." Jess paused. "No, after Grace arrived, after that I was so completely knocked sideways I could barely function. As I said, I tried to keep away so I could get things into perspective." She gave a crooked smile. "That plan didn't work. And last night, afterwards, I knew I'd allowed everything to get so out of my control, I guess I panicked. When Miranda rang about the dog it gave me a reality check." She looked down at her hands, "I freaked out and ran."

"Jess, it doesn't have to be so terrifying. I'd never do anything to upset your life or your family."

"My family." Jess gave a rueful laugh. "As you might have guessed I have an unconventional family. But it's far more unconventional than you know."

Kat remained silent. Did Jess mean she and Mark—?

"The night I came to dinner and rambled on about my life history I left a goodly part out. When I told you our story, Mark's and Lucas's and mine, I didn't tell you everything about the three of us. There was more.

"As I told you, when we were young we were like siblings. And then we grew up. Mark and I stayed together as a couple because it was easier that way. Deep down I knew it was easier for me. I had no desire to go out with anyone else. I accepted Mark as my boyfriend because I thought that was what I had to do. And Mark was familiar and safe."

Jess moved in her chair, brushed a strand of hair back behind her ear. "I did love Mark, but not the way I should have. The night before we got married I was so wound up I couldn't sleep. I kept thinking it was all wrong, that I was making a mistake. We never slept together before we were married. I never pushed the issue and neither did Mark. That should have told me something, shouldn't it?"

"With hindsight," Kat said gently.

"All that night before the wedding I kept soul-searching, asking myself if it was what I really wanted. I kept telling myself it was. I wanted a home and a family. Mark came a poor third. Deep down I knew I should call it off, but I didn't want to hurt Mark. So I went through with it." She shook her head again. "Our wedding night was a fiasco for us both, but we persevered." She looked across at Kat. "I was so unhappy. And so was Mark. I could see it, but I didn't know how to change it. Then I was pregnant with Miranda and things sort of relaxed. For us both."

Jess shook her head. "When Miranda was six months old I was at the gym and I met Leah. She was divorced, no kids, and quite open about being a lesbian. I was attracted to her. Long story short, we had an affair for three months. It made me come to terms with myself, why I couldn't be in love with Mark. I felt so guilty, though, Kat. I felt like I was cheating everyone I loved. I saw it as finding myself and losing Mark, our family.

"Then Leah was transferred interstate. She wanted me to go with her. I didn't. I don't regret that because I knew we weren't meant to be together, but on some level I do regret I didn't explain to Mark how I felt sooner than I did."

"It must have been really stressful for you."

Jess nodded. "I felt as though there were two of me, living two separate lives. The public me, happily married. And the private me that no one knew existed, preferring women, too terrified to act on those feelings, bottling it all up inside me. Then I got pregnant again. Looking back I often wonder how Caleb came to be because our sex life, Mark's and mine, was all but nonexistent. Mark worked long hours. I was at home with Miranda but doing the office work for Mark and his father.

"It all came crashing down the night Caleb was born. I was stressed and guilty and I went into labour early. I nearly lost Caleb, and I got it into my head it was all my fault, a punishment if you like, for who I was, what I'd done."

Kat murmured sympathetically.

"My hormones were out of whack. It was a difficult birth. My emotions were going crazy. I was a total mess. Mark and Lucas were both there, and I tried to calm myself down. I thought I'd succeeded but when we were alone in the room, just Mark, Lucas and I... I just... It all poured out of me. I told Mark I couldn't stay married to him, that it was so wrong of me, that he deserved someone who could love him completely. And I told him I was a lesbian. There was this awful silence and then"—a tear cascaded down Jess's cheek—"I realized Mark was crying, tears streaming down his face. I was devastated. He just stood there sobbing." Jess paused, dashed away her own tears.

"Would you like me to make more tea?" Kat asked. The tea Em had made them sat on the coffee table untouched and cold.

"No." Jess shook her head. "But thanks. I just have to get this out, Kat, because I need you to know. You see, when Mark broke down it was Lucas who went to him, held him, tried to soothe him. And I saw the way they looked at each other. I knew in that moment that Mark and Lucas loved each other."

Kat was astounded. Mark and Lucas? She'd suspected Lucas was gay but Mark? He was so— She stopped herself, admitting she was succumbing to stereotypical appearances the way most people did.

"When Mark got himself together we all just looked at each other. I was totally numb. I asked them how long it had been that way for them. Mark said he knew for certain the day Lucas's father had hit Lucas. He said he couldn't tell anyone, not even Lucas, because he was so terrified of his feelings, of being gay.

"When Lucas left to live in Melbourne, Mark thought he was over it. But when Lucas came back Mark said he knew he wasn't. He was even more horrified about his feelings for Lucas. He said he loved me too, and that he thought if he put his feelings for Lucas behind him, chose a normal life, he could change. So he asked me to marry him." Jess's lips twisted. "So we were both doing everything for the wrong reasons."

"Did Lucas know how Mark felt? Back then?" Kat asked and Jess nodded.

"Apparently Mark had his own reservations the night before our wedding. Lucas and Mark went out for a drink, supposedly to celebrate Mark's last night of freedom. They both got slightly drunk and Mark admitted to Lucas how he felt about him. Lucas said he felt the same about Mark. They were both frantic. I asked them why they allowed the wedding to go ahead, and they said they both loved me and didn't want to hurt me. And neither of them thought they could cope with a gay lifestyle."

"So they didn't have a relationship?"

Jess shook her head. "They swore they didn't. Lucas said he tried to keep away, but he kept coming back. They'd fought their attraction for the two years Mark and I were married. So, as it turned out, it wasn't just Mark and I who were unhappy. The three of us were. We all cried that night. Eventually I told them they had my blessing, that Mark and I would divorce and they could be together.

"It took another year for Mark to come to terms with us divorcing. By then Lucas was working with us. He moved in with us and they have their section in the house and I have mine. It's worked well and hasn't had too much of an impact on the kids. They accept the three of us as part of their family life. It was all in place while they were very young."

"Do your parents know?" Kat asked. She knew Jess had said her mother was still disappointed about the divorce, but she also recalled Jess mentioning that both sets of parents, although upset, were tolerant and accepting.

"Not officially. Mark and Lucas are still fairly closeted." She shrugged. "I suppose I am too. Didn't they say in the old days it was easier for women to hide. I do think our parents know on some level, but they haven't asked so we don't tell. We just want the kids to have a normal, steady life. When they're older we'll tell them. However, I think Mark totally underestimates kids today, and I think they're far more aware than he realizes. But the bottom line is they know we love them unconditionally. I think that's the most important thing."

Kat agreed. "What about you? I mean, apart from the woman at the gym, have you— Has there been anyone else?"

Jess shook her head. "I guess in my way I've been pretty closeted too, although I have some wonderfully supportive lesbian friends."

"Like Rachel and Quinn?" Kat put in and Jess nodded.

"There've been times I've really leaned all over them. Like now," Jess added apologetically and Kat raised her eyebrows. "I'd admitted to them that I was interested in you before the night of the barbecue. After that night they said they'd twigged you were a lesbian, and they thought you were interested in me too."

Kat smiled. "They were right."

"It did give me some small hope." She nervously brushed a strand of fair hair back behind her ear again. "Oh, Kat. You came along with your incredible dark eyes and, well, the wonderful all of you, and I fell like a ton of bricks. That first day. When I saw you standing there in the midst of the rubble of your house I knew things would never be the same for me.

"And when Meggie phoned you, and you smiled at the sound of her voice. My heart sank. I thought at first she was your partner, and I was so unbelievably disappointed. I wanted you to look at me like that."

"Like I'm looking at you now?" Kat asked softly.

Jess nodded. "But back then, just when I thought I was safe on the Meggie front, Em turned up."

Kat laughed. "Oh, yes. The ever incorrigible Em. She's the very best of best friends."

"I sort of got that impression. But then Meggie basically implied that you and her mother were an item. I even cried on Rachel's shoulder over that. They said they liked you very much, but they were concerned about the possibility that you were in a relationship with Meggie's mother. They didn't want me to get hurt. Their advice was for me to ask you straight out. But I was such a coward. I just couldn't bring myself to do it in case I wouldn't want to hear your answer."

"And I couldn't find a way to explain about Shael without outing myself and taking the chance you'd run off in terror."

"Did I look terrified?" Jess asked, exasperated, and Kat laughed.

"Not all the time. You were pretty cool mostly. I was pretty terrified, though, about how I felt about you. And I thought I was keeping my feelings for you under such good wraps. I was sure I was doing a more than adequate job of hiding it."

"You were. Most of the time." Jess grinned. "But occasionally I'd get a smidgen of a suspicion. It played havoc with my sleep patterns."

They laughed softly, then Kat sobered. "Jess, about Shael. We were together for ten years, and I thought I loved her. Looking back, I think I loved the person I wanted her to be. It was hardly Shael's fault that she wasn't that person. With hindsight I know I should have left years earlier. But I couldn't leave Meggie."

"I can understand that. Meggie loves you. That's so obvious."

"I love her too, and I'm hoping Shael and I can find some common ground with the custody issue."

They sat looking at each other. Kat was just happy to take in Jess sitting there, wanting to be there, knowing she felt the way Kat did. Part of her couldn't quite believe it, and she wanted Jess in her arms, to lay her ghosts, those old insecurity demons. "You know, Meggie keeps telling me how wonderful you are and how much she likes you."

"She does?"

Kat nodded.

"Miranda's the same about you. I wonder if… It's just that those two talk almost every night. I think it might explain something Miranda said to me after Caleb's party. She said, 'You know that Kat's a lesbian, Mum. Meggie told me. That means Kat likes to be with women. That's probably why she likes to be with you.' I was trying to come to terms with why I wanted to be with you too, so I wasn't exactly functioning to my full potential. I was so taken aback when Miranda said that I'm afraid I changed the subject really quickly. Lucas was there, and he walked off grinning like a Cheshire cat. I'm sure he made some comment about out of the mouth of babes."

Kat laughed too. "Do you think it's going to be a problem? Us, I mean?"

"No. I hope not. Not with Mark and Lucas I don't think. I guess I'll just have some talking to do. With the kids."

Kat nodded. "As I said, I really didn't want to cause any problems in your life, Jess," Kat began.

Jess stood up then, held out her hand and Kat took it. Jess pulled Kat to her feet and into her arms. "What I really want right now is to kiss you. Is that what you want too?"

Kat simply sank into Jess's arms, her lips finding Jess's. They kissed, slowly first, intoxicatingly slowly, and Kat drank in the softness of Jess's mouth, the heady wonder of the feel of her body close to hers. Then their kisses deepened until they drew apart, both breathless.

"I so needed that," Jess said. She glanced at the door Em had closed on her way out. "Shall we take advantage of the forward-thinking Em's decision to keep out intruders and any other stray women who might be passing and desperately feel the need to come right on in and kiss you too? Because I'm putting you on notice that I'll be keeping you so very busy doing just that you won't have time to kiss other women."

"Or the inclination," Kat promised.

"Wonderful. So shall we pick up where we left off last night?"

Kat gazed into Jess's eyes, seeing desire burning there, dropped her gaze to Jess's lips, those soft inviting lips. "Picking up where we left off last night? Now, that's amazing because that's just what I was thinking."

"Perfect." Jess kissed her again and Kat's knees almost gave out beneath her. "Remind me to thank Em. I know she did ask you to call her later, but if it's all right with you, do you think she'd mind if we left it till much, much later."

"I had the very same thoughts again," Kat said. "I think we're traveling in the same direction, don't you?"

"Mmm," Jess murmured against Kat's mouth. "Down the hall to that wonderful new bedroom of yours?"

"Oh, yes," said Kat and they moved towards the back of the house together. "Em sets a lot of store by forks in the road of life," Kat told Jess. "I think this time I've taken the best fork of my life. The road you're traveling on." She paused and Jess stopped, arm still holding her close. "I love you, Jess. So much. Do you think, well, that we'll—"

"I know we will. I love you too, Kat. I think from the first moment I saw you I loved you. And I've been waiting for you. Just you. To join me on that journey." She turned, held Kat's face in her hands. "I'm so going to enjoy our voyage together."

"But, what if —"

Jess kissed her. Deeply. "Discovering each other is going to be part of that wonderful journey, don't you think?" She looked into Kat's eyes. "I can't promise we won't have ruts in that road, my love, but the getting there, well, the getting there is going to be incredible, amazing, exhilarating!" She laughed softly as she took Kat's hand and they moved forward together.

**Publications from
Bella Books, Inc.**
Women. Books. Even Better Together.
**P.O. Box 10543
Tallahassee, FL 32302
Phone: 800-729-4992
www.bellabooks.com**

CALM BEFORE THE STORM by Peggy J. Herring. Colonel Marcel Robideaux doesn't tell and so far no one official has asked, but the amorous pursuit by Jordan McGowan has her worried for both her career and her honor.
978-0-9677753-1-9

THE WILD ONE by Lyn Denison. Rachel Weston is busy keeping home and head together after the death of her husband. Her kids need her and what she doesn't need is the confusion that Quinn Farrelly creates in her body and heart.
978-0-9677753-4-0

LESSONS IN MURDER by Claire McNab. There's a corpse in the school with a neat hole in the head and a Black & Decker drill alongside. Which teacher should Inspector Carol Ashton suspect? Unfortunately, the alluring Sybil Quade is at the top of the list. First in this highly lauded series.
978-1-931513-65-4

WHEN AN ECHO RETURNS by Linda Kay Silva. The bayou where Echo Branson found her sanity has been swept clean by a hurricane — or at least they thought. Then an evil washed up by the storm comes looking for them all, one-by-one. Second in series.
978-1-59493-225-0

DEADLY INTERSECTIONS by Ann Roberts. Everyone is lying, including her own father and her girlfriend. Leaving matters to the professionals is supposed to be easier! Third in series with *PAID IN FULL* and *WHITE OFFERINGS*.
978-1-59493-224-3

SUBSTITUTE FOR LOVE by Karin Kallmaker. No substitutes, ever again! But then Holly's heart, body and soul are captured by Reyna... Reyna with no last name and a secret life that hides a terrible bargain, one written in family blood.
978-1-931513-62-3

MAKING UP FOR LOST TIME by Karin Kallmaker. Take one Next Home Network Star and add one Little White Lie to equal mayhem in little Mendocino and a recipe for sizzling romance. This lighthearted, steamy story is a feast for the senses in a kitchen that is way too hot.
978-1-931513-61-6

2ND FIDDLE by Kate Calloway. Cassidy James's first case left her with a broken heart. At least this new case is fighting the good fight, and she can throw all her passion and energy into it.
978-1-59493-200-7

HUNTING THE WITCH by Ellen Hart. The woman she loves — used to love — offers her help, and Jane Lawless finds it hard to say no. She needs TLC for recent injuries and who better than a doctor? But Julia's jittery demeanor awakens Jane's curiosity. And Jane has never been able to resist a mystery. #9 in series and Lammy-winner.
978-1-59493-206-9

FAÇADES by Alex Marcoux. Everything Anastasia ever wanted — she has it. Sidney is the woman who helped her get it. But keeping it will require a price — the unnamed passion that simmers between them.
978-1-59493-239-7

ELENA UNDONE by Nicole Conn. The risks. The passion. The devastating choices. The ultimate rewards. Nicole Conn rocked the lesbian cinema world with Claire of the Moon and has rocked it again with Elena Undone. This is the book that tells it all...
978-1-59493-254-0

WHISPERS IN THE WIND by Frankie J. Jones. It began as a camping trip, then a simple hike. Dixon Hayes and Elizabeth Colter uncover an intriguing cave on their hike, changing their world, perhaps irrevocably.
978-1-59493-037-9

WEDDING BELL BLUES by Julia Watts. She'll do anything to save what's left of her family. Anything. It didn't seem like a bad plan...at first. Hailed by readers as Lammy-winner Julia Watts' funniest novel.
978-1-59493-199-4

WILDFIRE by Lynn James. From the moment botanist Devon McKinney meets ranger Elaine Thomas the chemistry is undeniable. Sharing — and protecting — a mountain for the length of their short assignments leads to unexpected passion in this sizzling romance by newcomer Lynn James.
978-1-59493-191-8

LEAVING L.A. by Kate Christie. Eleanor Chapin is on the way to the rest of her life when Tessa Flanaghan offers her a lucrative summer job caring for Tessa's daughter Laya. It's only temporary and everyone expects Eleanor to be leaving L.A...
978-1-59493-221-2

SOMETHING TO BELIEVE by Robbi McCoy. When Lauren and Cassie meet on a once-in-a-lifetime river journey through China their feelings are innocent...at first. Ten years later, nothing — and everything — has changed. From Golden Crown winner Robbi McCoy.
978-1-59493-214-4

DEVIL'S ROCK by Gerri Hill. Deputy Andrea Sullivan and Agent Cameron Ross vow to bring a killer to justice. The killer has other plans. Gerri Hill pens another intriguing blend of mystery and romance in this page-turning thriller.
978-1-59493-218-2

SHADOW POINT by Amy Briant. Madison Maguire has just been not-quite fired, told her brother is dead and discovered she has to pick up a five-year old niece she's never met. After she makes it to Shadow Point it seems like someone—or something—doesn't want her to leave. Romance sizzles in this ghost story from Amy Briant.
978-1-59493-216-8

JUKEBOX by Gina Daggett. Debutantes in love. With each other. Two young women chafe at the constraints of parents and society with a friendship that could be more, if they can break free. Gina Daggett is best known as "Lipstick" of the columnist duo Lipstick & Dipstick.
978-1-59493-212-0

BLIND BET by Tracey Richardson. The stakes are high when Ellen Turcotte and Courtney Langford meet at the blackjack tables. Lady Luck has been smiling on Courtney but Ellen is a wild card she may not be able to handle.
978-1-59493-211-3